CONTENTS

THE COURT PAINTER'S APPRENTICE

Richard Knight

First published in Great Britain in 2012
by Catnip Publishing Ltd
This Large Print edition published 2012
by AudioGO Ltd
by arrangement with
Catnip Publishing Ltd

ISBN: 978 1445 848884

British Library Cataloguing in Publication Data available

Printed and bound in Great Britain by
MPG Books Group Limited

PROLOGUE

Take a look in a mirror.

What do you see? A nose that's too large, or skin marked with freckles like paint splashes from a brush? Perhaps eyes that seem sunken and dark, an expression of gloom baked hard on the mouth? Whatever you see, staring at your reflection for too long is rarely a comfortable experience for all but the fairest of us. We prefer only fleeting glimpses of ourselves, long enough to brush our hair or wash our faces.

Now, take a closer look.

Wait until you are completely alone and the house is quiet. Focus on your eyes. Let your mind go blank and sink deep into yourself. It takes time but sooner or later, perhaps only for a second or two, you are suddenly staring at the face of a complete stranger. It's an intense and unsettling experience but it soon passes and the old, familiar features return. However, in that brief moment you have seen a strange

1

part of yourself break away from the whole. Not that tired face you see every morning, but something, someone, you have never set eyes on before.

Don't stay like that for too long; who knows what it would lead to.

JOHANN

The innkeeper nodded at the window as he placed a mug of ale next to the soup. 'A foul evening, sir,' he said.

'Certainly,' Hugo replied, taking a spoonful of the soup. It was good and hearty, full of meat and vegetables. 'Thank you.'

'You're most welcome. Have you ridden far today, sir?' the innkeeper asked.

'From Bruges,' Hugo replied, happy to pass the time in friendly conversation. 'I have been discussing a new painting at the town hall there.'

The innkeeper nodded thoughtfully, wiping his hands on his apron. 'So, you are an artist?'

'Yes, I have a workshop in Ghent.'

There was a short silence as Hugo ate a little more soup. The inn was a travellers' inn, two miles from the nearest village, and on such a wild night it was almost deserted. Three men sat together in a corner deep in conversation, pipe smoke obscuring their faces from Hugo's failing sight.

He had found the inn by chance. As the rain in his face had grown faster, whipping in from the sea across the flat fields, he had sheltered with his horse under a tree and from there he noticed the lights in the windows of a building half a mile further along the road. Now that he was warm once more and enjoying a good meal and company he had no intention of leaving until the next morning. He was not expected at home until tomorrow evening. Better to stay here tonight and surprise his wife, Magdalena, by arriving at lunchtime the next day.

'Ah, the soup is good. Very good indeed,' Hugo said.

The innkeeper smiled politely. 'Thank you. Your room is ready, sir. Tell me when you wish to see it.' Then he walked slowly back behind the counter and began to dry some mugs.

As a child, high up in his father's studio that looked out over the plains of Flanders, Hugo had stared for hours at a mirror, striving for a

4

glimpse of his soul. Now, fifty years later, sitting in this Flemish inn with rain streaming down the windows, he recalled those early days when he first began searching for the true portrait of a person. Not just a simple likeness. Nothing annoyed him more than some merchant's wife squealing: 'It looks just like him!' No, what Hugo had always longed for, more than anything else, was to know that he had painted a true person; to hear the words 'it *is* him'. Now he was beginning to slow down, painting no more than two hours early in the morning to catch the light. His eyes grew tired quickly these days, but from time to time he would still hold up his mirror and look for that stranger, as though he were still a boy of ten in his father's studio.

The food, ale and the warmth of the roaring fire had made him sleepy, and Hugo was about to retire to bed when something caught his attention. On a wooden shelf next to his table was a small piece of white paper propped against the wall. Hugo leaned forward to focus his eyes better. On the paper

5

was a drawing—probably charcoal and chalk, he thought—of a man's face. He instantly recognised the large, heavy-set features of the innkeeper.

The drawing was magnificent. There was a confidence in the line and shading which made Hugo think this must be the work of an experienced artist, perhaps someone like himself, passing through the countryside. The skin, even in simple charcoal, had real texture, and the eyes . . . ! It was a rare achievement to have created the life that sparkled from those eyes with such a simple tool.

He signalled for the innkeeper to come over. The man approached, wiping his hands on his apron, expecting an order for more ale or soup.

'Sir, I couldn't help but admire this fine drawing of you, here on the shelf.' The innkeeper nodded and smiled. 'It is a portrait drawn by a skilful artist, I believe. Tell me, who drew it?'

The innkeeper's smile broadened as Hugo spoke. He stood there, struck dumb for a second or two but clearly delighted. Hugo suddenly realised that maybe he had just complimented the artist himself.

'Surely not a self-portrait? I must say, sir, you draw with such skill . . .'

The innkeeper raised his hand to stop Hugo, laughing quietly. 'I'm sorry. I am so pleased you have noticed the portrait, but *I* didn't draw it.'

'Then who *did*?' Hugo was intrigued. He knew many artists in Flanders, but the style of this portrait was unique.

'Johann!' The innkeeper turned to the counter as he called. A head appeared round the doorframe to the kitchen beyond, from where the soup had come. But where Hugo expected to see an adult, was the face of a boy no more than eleven years old. He had a happy, open expression and a thick head of dark hair. 'Come, Johann. Come and meet an admirer!'

The boy stepped shyly from behind the counter and approached Hugo's table.

'Well, well. You must be . . .' Hugo began.

'Yes, sir. He is my only son.' The

7

innkeeper placed his arm around Johann's shoulders.

'And you drew this portrait of your father, did you, Johann?' Hugo continued, in a kindly voice. The boy nodded cautiously. 'It is a fine likeness. I suppose you have a good teacher?'

The boy looked a little confused for a moment. 'No, sir. I don't go to school. But I can read and write a little.'

Hugo laughed gently. 'No, no. I mean somebody must have taught you to draw like this. Who was it?'

The innkeeper interrupted. 'He has never been taught, sir. I gave him charcoal as a small child and what little paper I could afford. But no, sir, he has never had a lesson, though he spends hours in his room at practice.'

This was truly incredible. Hugo leaned back in his chair and looked intently at the man and his son, but there was no deception in their smiling eyes. After a lifetime of studying faces Hugo would have been able to spot it straightaway. It was at that moment when, suddenly, an idea arrived in his head, fully formed. Before he'd had time to consider it, he was already speaking his mind.

'Tell me, sir. What plans do you have for your son and his talents?'

The innkeeper looked embarrassed. 'I had always thought he would follow me in my trade and take over the inn one day.'

'And his drawing?' Hugo asked.

The innkeeper hesitated before speaking. 'Well, I'm sure *you* do well, sir. But for Johann I don't think there is much money to be gained in drawing pictures.'

How wrong he was! Hugo knew that with such a talent, and a few years training in oils, there was a great future for the boy.

'Tell me, Johann. Do you love to draw?' Hugo asked.

Johann's eyes suddenly burned with passion, his voice clearer and bolder as he answered. 'I do, sir. It makes me happy. I feel so alive, but calm too . . . and a little sad sometimes. I can't explain . . .' Johann's voice trailed away as his eyes were drawn to the fire.

Hugo got up, moved his chair along

9

and pulled two more around the table. 'Come, sit with me. Let's talk about painting.' The innkeeper and his son looked at each other briefly, and sat down. 'You know, Johann, I've painted so many portraits I can scarcely remember them all!'

Johann smiled at Hugo. 'Who have you painted?' he asked eagerly.

'Merchants, rich families, guildsmen, court officials, princes even. Twenty years ago I was court painter to the Emperor in Brussels, no less.'

Johann's dark eyes widened and his mouth dropped open. 'The Emperor?' he whispered.

'Yes, the Emperor,' Hugo laughed and ruffled Johann's hair.

The innkeeper laughed, too. 'Well, we are in good company here, eh, Johann?' he said.

Johann smiled and nodded, hoping for more information about this painter.

Hugo took a sip of his ale and then continued. 'I still paint portraits from time to time but I leave most of the background detail to my assistants

10

these days. I am too old, and my eyesight is fading fast. My children are all grown up and have gone to find their own way in the world. You know, it's funny. Not one of them had the slightest interest in painting.' Hugo sighed briefly, looking at the rain streaming down the window, then picked up Johann's drawing of his father. 'But then, it's really not something that can be forced.' He looked a little longer at the drawing before turning to Johann's father. 'I have a proposition for you.'

And so it was that Hugo offered to take Johann as an apprentice at his workshop in Ghent. This was Hugo's chance to pass on all his experience and skill to someone who he suspected would care more about his art than money.

At first the innkeeper remained quiet and listened thoughtfully. But when Hugo described the life that Johann might one day lead, thirty miles away in Ghent, he hurried off to fetch his wife.

Whilst the boy's father was gone,

11

Hugo talked to Johann quietly. 'You have been blessed with a rare gift, Johann. I can help you to use it wisely . . . if you want me to, that is. But learn one thing here and now, before anything else. An artist must hold up a mirror to the world. Many artists will paint what they are asked to paint, by whoever commissions them. They are happy to change what they see to suit the merchants and burghers who pay them. But to me those painters are just workmen—as happy to paint a shop sign as a portrait. Truth is more important, Johann. Be true to what you see.'

Johann listened politely, but really he didn't understand what Hugo was talking about. All he knew was that his life was changing quickly, all in the course of one stormy winter evening.

Johann's mother wept softly as a plan was worked out between Hugo and her husband. The whole family was to be brought to Ghent in two weeks to meet Hugo and his wife in their home. Once there they could reassure themselves that Johann's future would be both safe and happy.

'The apprenticeship will be for three years,' Hugo explained. 'Johann can visit you every second Sunday. I will pay his guild fees and he can begin in the workshop preparing the panels and the paints. When I have time he will draw and learn to paint with me, as long as he is still happy in my house. I will teach him all I know. And mark my words! One day he may be a famous painter. What do you say, Johann?'

Johann looked at his mother and father. They smiled sadly and nodded to him, for they knew this was an opportunity which they would all be fools to miss. He looked back at Hugo.

'Thank you, sir. I would be happy to accept your generous invitation.'

THE WORKSHOP

Hugo's workshop was at the back of a tall house in the middle of Ghent.

'This is where you will work for the first year. The men will show you what to do,' Hugo said as he showed Johann round.

The workshop was three times the size of an ordinary room. It was furnished with two central rows of wooden workbenches and several easels scattered in the corners, each holding a portrait or a religious panel. Some were only sketched out in charcoal, ink, or red ochre—which Johann later found out was Hugo's favourite. Other panels were painted, but only with what looked to Johann like blobs of dark colours.

'That is the underpainting, Johann. To show the dark areas of the portrait,' Hugo explained. Johann peered at one of the portraits and was astounded to see the faint image of a face peering back from under the formless paint.

'Here, look. This one is almost finished. Another week or two and it will be dry and ready to varnish.' Hugo pulled him over to an easel where there was a small portrait of an elegant man and his wife who were standing in front of a table laden with cherries, a loaf of bread and a vase of flowers. Johann stood, taking in every detail.

'That is the first secretary of the Grand Council and his wife,' Hugo told him. Johann did not know who such people were, although he was interested in the expressions on their faces.

They do not care for each other, he thought to himself, but said nothing in case he should offend Hugo.

Johann was quiet in the company of the older men, who frightened him a little, making jokes he couldn't understand. Every day he worked with them in the workshop, learning to coat the oak panels with plaster ground and glue. He learned to grind and mix the pigments that the apothecary's boy delivered in paper packets, and one of Johann's jobs was to empty them into the clay pots lined on the shelves at the side of the workshop. He did it slowly, so that he could study the different colours; lead white, bone black, red vermilion. The blue azurite startled Johann the first time he saw it. He had never seen a colour so rich and bright.

'What are you playing at, Johann?' someone would shout. 'Don't take all day about it!'

'No, not like that,' said one of the men, snatching the stone pestle from Johann as he attempted to grind some bone black for the first time. He watched as the man showed him again, raising his shoulder to put all his bodyweight behind the grinding. 'Come on. You'd better build up those muscles,' he cried, and the other men laughed at the joke. Johann turned away, embarrassed, and tried again. But somehow he could not make the powder as fine as the man had.

Johann was shown how to bind the powdered pigment with linseed oil to make the paint, and to thin it with turpentine when needed. He loved the way the oil and pigment bound

16

together slowly. He had never seen paint before and often sneaked a finger in to feel its cool, silky texture.

Hugo was often away from the workshop visiting his patrons or at the guildhall. Johann didn't like being left alone with the men. They treated him well enough, but they were not apprentices like him. They were not boys either. They were men and they lived in their own houses with their own families in another part of the city.

'You are lucky, boy,' one of the men said, as they gathered one lunchtime around the fire at the end of the workshop to eat bread and cheese. 'We did not think the master would take another apprentice.' He smiled and pinched Johann's cheek. Johann noticed how the man's fingers were stained a brownish yellow from the earth pigments.

During those first winter afternoons, Johann longed for the light in the workshop to fade so he could return upstairs to Hugo's wife, Magdalena. She soon loved Johann as though he was her own child. She saw in his eyes

17

how hard it was for him to be away from his family for two whole weeks. So she spent as much time with him as she could. In the long evenings she helped him with his reading and writing. The wind from the North Sea was the music that accompanied Johann's education. As the candles guttered in the draughts that sliced through every crack in the house, Johann peered at the letters and learned quickly from a patient teacher.

'You miss your mother, Johann. I can tell,' she said one evening when he couldn't concentrate on his reading. She stroked his hair and he leaned in a little against her shoulder.

'Yes,' he replied. 'But I am very happy to be here, madam. You have both been so kind to me.' Johann was anxious not to appear ungrateful.

'Shhh.' Magdalena patted his head. 'Don't call me "madam". It makes me feel old. Magdalena will do.' Johann looked up at her face and she smiled. 'Come, put your book away.'

Johann followed Magdalena down to the kitchen where she prepared warm milk and bread for him. Johann studied her face bathed in the glow from the fire. It was a face he was quickly growing to know and love like his own mother's; every line, every shadow, every blemish, the way kindness flooded across her skin when she smiled, the grey hairs that fell loose from her lace cap.

One Saturday a few weeks later, Hugo sent the men home early for the afternoon.

'Come!' he said to Magdalena and Johann. 'Get your cloaks. We are going out.'

It was the first time Johann had left the workshop or the house since his arrival in Ghent. The day was bright and cold as they strode down the cobbled street away from the house. Johann was amazed by the constant noise around him, the rumble of cartwheels and the clipping of horses' hooves on the stone. He had never been to a town or a city before, although he had heard travellers at his father's inn describe the great cities of Bruges, Brussels and Antwerp. He watched every face that rushed past them, looking for someone familiar, but of course they were all strangers. As they reached the market square and headed down a street towards the river, Johann was warned to keep close to Hugo, and Magdalena held his arm tightly as they threaded their way through the jostling bodies.

'That is the painters' guildhall, Johann; the Guild of St Luke,' Hugo said, pointing at a large stone building facing the river. Johann noticed how the gable ends were stepped, as though you could climb up the roof. 'One day, when you are eighteen, you will pay your fees and become a master painter of Ghent there.'

Johann stared at the building as though it possessed some mystical hold over him. This was the place that had the power to make him a true artist. His eyes scanned the tiny sculpted figures around the large oak door and Johann decided, there and then, that one day he would walk down the steps from that door as a master painter.

'Come, this way,' Hugo said, tugging Johann's sleeve and snapping him out of his daydream. 'I have something I want you to see.'

They made their way along the river, through the mud and hay and manure that carpeted the cobbles, then turned back into the city. Hugo led them this way and that, down narrow alleyways where Johann held his breath because the smell was so bad, then suddenly out onto a wide street again. Johann stopped amongst the crowd and Magdalena, almost bumping into Johann, called Hugo back.

'The church of St Bavo. Magnificent, eh?' Hugo said, seeing Johann's neck tilting back to take in the tower before them. To Johann it was the most wonderful sight. Of course he had seen country churches before, but he had never imagined a building so tall. Its four turrets seemed to point up to the blue sky, to heaven even, Johann thought.

'Come, let's go in and have a look,' Hugo said, taking Johann's arm and leading him towards the huge arched doors. Johann could not move his eyes from the carved stone images above

21

them. It must have taken years to build something so large, so beautiful, so intricate. Hugo saw Johann looking at the figures and smiled at Magdalena.

'See how he looks? I told you. A born artist,' he whispered in her ear.

They went inside where Johann's eyes swept slowly across the enormous vaulted roof above them. If anything it felt even colder inside the church. A strange stillness seeped through the church's gloom and Johann was only faintly aware of the street noises beyond the thick stone walls. At the door, Hugo spoke to a man who led them down the aisle then towards a small chapel where he opened the door with a key.

Inside the chapel Johann saw a large, hinged wooden panel painted with wonderful scenes. Sunlight streamed through an east window, deepening the colours and adding a glow that contrasted with the dark coolness of the nave. His heart beat heavily as he took in the details; the depth of the central panel where his eyes were drawn away from a lamb standing on an altar towards a castle and city in the background.

Hugo and Magdalena stood back for a long time as Johann wandered up and down the panels. The detail was so fine that Johann saw every tiny jewel in the hems of the robes, the veins in the feet of the worshippers and the smallest of pebbles on the ground.

'So what can you see?' Hugo asked after several minutes. Johann looked up for the first time, seeming almost surprised that Hugo was still there.

'Great beauty,' he whispered. 'I have never . . .' but his voice trailed off, lost in the peace of the chapel, as his eyes were pulled back to the painting again. Slowly, Hugo took Johann along the painting pointing out Adam and Eve on the small side panels, the angels playing musical instruments and the Holy Trinity with God the Father at the centre.

'What?' Johann gasped. 'Is that God? How does he know what God looks like?'

Hugo laughed. 'He doesn't, Johann. He has imagined it.'

Hugo continued, helping Johann see the smaller details—the sheen of the brocades worn by the angels or the folds of St John's green cloak. They were there for an hour or more.

'Haven't you two seen enough now?' Magdalena complained but when Hugo and Johann turned to her she was chuckling as she shook her head.

'So, Johann, you have seen great art today. Never mind my silly portraits. This was a man who could paint with the beauty of God in his hands. Jan van Eyck,' Hugo said as they walked out into the daylight again. 'I only wish I had gifts such as his. Maybe you will paint something like that one day, if you practise long and hard, and dedicate yourself to your work. True art takes time and patience, Johann. Remember that. It must have taken years to paint such a masterpiece.'

Johann squinted in the bright sunlight. 'Thank you for showing me. It was wonderful.'

After a month or two, the assistants seemed to accept Johann, although they muttered under their breath when

24

Hugo took him up to the studio at the top of the house. Each afternoon, Hugo would sit for an hour and watch Johann sketch, offering advice and encouragement.

When six months had passed, Hugo was confident enough of Johann's model sketches to allow him to help with the underdrawing for a painting of an Italian banker, Signor Portinari, who lived in Bruges. When he had finished, the men in the workshop stood behind Johann looking at the drawing sketched out on the white, coated panel.

'Well, it's as good as yours, if not better, Pieter!' one of the men said.

By copying some of Hugo's smaller original paintings, Johann soon developed an understanding of colour. Hugo taught Johann to build layers of paint from thin to thick to stop the portrait from cracking and Johann patiently studied Hugo's methods for drying the many layers in his paintings. On the rare occasions when Johann made a mistake, Hugo would supervise the scraping away of a layer of paint before it dried.

In the mornings, Hugo and Johann would sometimes stand together at the door of the workshop watching the clouds, finding images there as they shifted and shaped themselves in the sky. Johann soon knew that you couldn't paint the Flanders sky with only simple grey. Sometimes the clouds loosened and drifted and shafts of sunlight would pierce the air of the workshop. Behind them, the men grumbled as they sanded another panel, or painted another background colour.

'Look at the dust, Johann,' Hugo said one afternoon as lines of light from the setting sun arrowed in through the studio window. 'Describe it to me.'

Johann looked carefully at the tiny particles swirling in the light, thickening its glow. 'It's like it makes the light move. Like it has its own body now!'

Hugo laughed and patted Johann's back. 'And what does it make you think of?' he asked.

'Melting butter. Or honey,' Johann replied quickly.

Hugo made Johann study his own face in a mirror, in different lights at different times of the day, and practise mixing colours to match. And somewhere in that studio, at some time or other when Johann was too busy to notice, they became friends who were at ease with the silence that often sat between them as they worked.

Early one summer morning before the men arrived, as the sun rose over the fields and began to colour the workshop walls, Hugo hid behind a screen and watched Johann adding brushstrokes to a portrait of a Spanish court official. With any other apprentice he might have been angered by the boy's impudence but with Johann it didn't seem so wrong. Hugo, his eyes now severely clouded, was sure that one day Johann would be a better painter than him, better indeed than any painter he had ever known. After watching the boy use Alizarin crimson to alter the tone of skin on the official's cheekbone, reflecting the light entering the window, Hugo smiled and crept silently away leaving Johann to clean his brushes, unaware that he had been observed.

Month by month Johann slowly grew used to his new life as a painter's apprentice. Every other Sunday he went home to the inn with one of Hugo's servants, returning to Ghent early the next morning. The inn itself began to fill up with examples of Johann's copies of Hugo's miniature portraits and his reputation amongst the customers was now considerable. Johann had already been allowed to paint some background sections of Hugo's larger portraits and no longer spent as much time with the men grinding pigments. Hugo had even let Johann paint a portrait of a merchant's son on his own. The merchant had agreed with the Guild to pay a smaller price if Johann was given charge of the painting. The boy would not sit still for long but Johann finished plenty of sketches and only called him to sit twice more. The moment he first began to add the flesh tones and the face took on some form of life, he shivered with excitement

When Hugo looked at Johann's first finished painting of the merchant's son he simply smiled to himself, satisfied at the thought of the great talent he was bringing to the world, and congratulated himself on his instincts that cold night at the inn over a year ago. Johann painted, naturally and without any teaching, a person's soul.

And Hugo always offered Johann the same advice: 'Paint what you see, Johann; not what you think you see.'

THE SPICE MERCHANT'S WIFE

Johann had barely turned thirteen when one day the wife of a wealthy spice merchant called Van Melen sat in front of him, looking ill and gloomy.

As he prepared some studies for her portrait, he saw how her downcast eyes were banked by shadows and her skin was the colour of sour milk. Johann felt sorry for her and tried to talk as he worked. She seemed shy.

'Your husband, he is a spice merchant, madam?' Johann tried, politely.

She smiled weakly at him. 'Yes. From Antwerp. But he prefers to live here in Ghent.' Then she said little else for the rest of the sitting.

The next day she was a little less reserved and asked to see the drawings before she left. Johann was reluctant.

'Would it not be better to wait until I paint you, madam? There is so much work to be done yet, you may be disappointed in what you see,' he

30

lied. In truth, he knew he had drawn her just as he saw her—unhappy and unhealthy.

But the spice merchant's wife gently insisted. So Johann passed her his book and as she flicked through the pages she let out a little whimper.

'Surely not? Is that really me? Am I truly so miserable?' she exclaimed.

'No, no, as I tried to tell you . . .' Johann began. But he stopped short as he watched a tear build in the corner of her eye and flow down her sallow cheek.

It was several weeks before the spice merchant's wife returned again for Johann to organise the composition. Hugo was confident enough in Johann's skills to leave the details to him on many of their paintings now, although he would inspect each stage of a painting and make suggestions. His fading eyesight was a problem and he spent very little time in the workshop now. The woman sat down in the window seat of the studio and gazed across the fields.

'Perhaps you would like to remain

seated there for your portrait? You look . . .' Johann searched for a word that could not offend her. 'Thoughtful.'

She looked at him and smiled. 'Yes, of course. The window seat it shall be. And how shall I arrange my gown?'

Johann helped her fold the cloth carefully and placed her hands in her lap, fingers locked together. Then he shifted her a little so that she was slightly to one side of the window. That way, he could still paint part of the window and show the light reflecting on the wall next to it. He directed her gaze slightly downwards and away from the easel, making a chalk mark on the wall behind for her to look at. Finally, Johann was satisfied.

As he began sketching on the sanded white panel, with bold, confident strokes in red ochre, her face again began to take on a certain sadness. Johann could not help it. It was the way she looked. Hugo would tell him that you must draw and paint what you see.

'How is your husband?' Johann asked as he sketched.

'Very well thank you, Johann. He

has gone away on business to England today. He wanted to know how the portrait was coming along, but I told him what you told me. Good art takes time.' She smiled, and just for a second Johann detected a little colour in her face.

'Do you have children?' Johann continued, glad that she was able to talk to him more freely. It was several seconds before he glanced up from his drawing and noticed what effect his words had had on her.

'My husband is a generous man,' she said, a tear rolling down her cheek. 'He gives me everything . . . everything I could wish for. There is nothing more I could ask of him as a husband. In return he asks only for a child and that is the one thing I cannot give him.'

Johann was not sure how to reply. He had not expected his question to cause such pain. The woman looked out of the window, watching the shadows of clouds race each other across the fields towards the house.

A month later Johann sent a note to the spice merchant's wife to ask her to sit again now that the underpainting had been done. Down in the workshop there were fewer men employed now that Hugo was barely painting anything himself. They painted signs and banners for processions mostly—and some backgrounds for Johann's portraits, although he preferred whenever he could to paint them himself.

'You must learn to trust the men, Johann. You cannot do everything yourself in a busy workshop, you know?' Hugo had said when he found Johann in the workshop painting a black background to a portrait of Signor Portinari's daughter.

Johann knew Hugo was a fine artist who still had much to teach him, but he had started to think differently about painting since taking on his own portraits. During his time in Ghent, Johann had been back many times to see the altarpiece in the church and could look at it for hours on end, finding new detail each time. Surely a painter would need to be in control of every last detail to produce something of such beauty? It was *his* imagination and nobody else's. Hugo let the assistants paint robes and backgrounds, based on his instructions, and then sold the portraits as his own. But Johann was not so sure this was the right way. He wanted to be an artist, not just a painter.

The men in the workshop began to grumble but were careful not to say anything too openly for fear of losing their jobs. They had watched how close Johann and Hugo had become. 'He won't be happy till we're all gone, and he can do everything himself!' Johann overheard one of the men say just as he was about to enter the workshop one afternoon.

'He's young. He'll soon learn that he needs us. The master will tell him,' another man replied. Johann coughed loudly before he walked through the door and the men turned back to the pigment they were grinding.

The spice merchant's wife sat, in the same clothes as before, by the window. Johann hardly ever painted in the workshop now. He preferred the light

35

and space of the studio at the top of the house, where he could watch the shadows of the clouds on the fields beyond the city.

'Your husband is still in England, madam?' he asked, painting the first flesh tones on the face and neck.

'Yes, although I expect him back within a week or two.'

'You will be glad to have him home safe again,' Johann continued, politely.

'Yes. I have missed him. I have enjoyed coming here to sit for you though. It has helped to pass the time a little.' She smiled at Johann, then looked back to her mark on the wall.

Johann nodded. 'Madam, it is my pleasure. The next few weeks I will paint your face. Much of the rest can be done without your presence. Will you be able to give me a day or two each week?'

'Of course.'

As the face on the panel took shape and life in layer after layer of paint, the spice merchant's wife became more and more curious.

'Can I see yet?' she asked. But

Johann politely declined. In truth, he was worried that she might not like it—he had painted her perfectly, with such paleness on her face and sadness in her eyes.

One day in the new year, as Johann began to put the finishing touches to the face, the woman came to sit for the last time.

'My husband returned yesterday, Johann,' she said, finding the mark on the wall as he arranged her gown.

'Ah, good. Did he have a successful trip?' Johann asked as he worked on mixing the right colour for the shadowed skin beneath her eyes.

The woman chatted happily about her husband's stories of life in London, the new contacts he had made and the stranger habits of the English. An hour passed quickly, then another, as they talked and Johann worked. He was pleased that she enjoyed her visits to his studio. Most people hated sitting still for so long.

As the light in the studio began to fade, Johann stood up and stretched.

'Well, madam. I think you are free

now! The rest I can manage without you here. It will take another month at least for me to finish the painting. Then it must dry thoroughly, and be glazed. In the meantime, tell your husband he is welcome to come and inspect it.'

'Am I not to see it?' she teased. Johann was glad to see her smiling, but was still unsure if she would like her portrait.

'Well, I suppose . . .'

She jumped up quickly, excited to see herself on the panel. As she came round to Johann's side however, her smile fell quickly away.

'Do I really look like that?' She looked up at him as she spoke and there was a deep sadness in her eyes. *It would be a challenge to paint those eyes as I see them now*, Johann thought to himself. He felt a strong urge to help this poor woman, but he didn't know what he could do or say to remove her feeling of despair.

'No. No—there's still much work to be done. Come back next month and you will have a more accurate portrait.' The words had flown from his lips without a thought.

She smiled as she left. 'Please, don't think badly of me. I didn't mean to be ungrateful. The portrait is just like me. You can only paint what you see.'

That evening Johann sat in the studio and thought about the woman. He could not help but feel a deep sympathy for her and wished there was some way he could help her. Over the next few weeks, Johann could think only of the portrait of the spice merchant's wife. He spent each day locked away in the attic studio, ignoring the men in the workshop downstairs.

The day before Van Melen's wife was due to return Johann sat well into the night, working as though possessed by a spirit he could not contain. With vermilion he added touches of colour to the woman's cheeks to give her youth and health. With azurite and a rich helping of boiled linseed oil and pine resin, he gave her gown a sumptuous blue sheen. He teased a smile onto her face. Johann didn't hear the storm raging in the night, out over the sea. The rain slicing through the darkness and rattling the glass was nothing to him. He worked furiously until dawn, when the first chords of light from the east stroked the portrait to life. Johann sat back and watched as the woman grew in health and confidence before his eyes. Finally, before retiring to his bed, he added a mirror on the wall behind her shoulder, reflecting the back of her head and a tiny, faint image of himself, the artist, which few would notice.

The next morning, the woman sat in the studio window behind the covered panel. The storm last night had kept her awake but she did not feel any tiredness. If anything she felt happier, at ease with the lightened world that she looked out on.

Johann appeared and apologised for his lateness.

'No matter. It's a wonderful morning. I was just admiring it from your window.' She smiled, and Johann couldn't help returning the smile. She looked so radiant and warm, framed by the morning sunlight behind her, such a contrast to her previous visits.

'Well! I hope you like what you see today and that it pleases your husband. I have worked long into the night to complete it.' Johann lifted the covering slowly. 'Come. See what you really look like!'

The woman edged round cautiously. But on seeing the portrait she almost leapt with delight and clapped her hands.

'Johann! It is . . . it is . . .' She could not find a word to fit.

'How you would like to be?' Johann suggested.

'Yes.' She sat down again with a large smile fixed on her lips.

'You must return in two weeks when the glaze is dry. Bring your husband, too. I'm sure he is desperate to see it.'

When Van Melen and his wife were shown into the studio, she could hardly keep still with excitement. Van Melen was a tall, sharp-featured man dressed in an expensive wool cloak with a spotted fur collar. He nodded politely as he entered the room. Johann shook hands with him and bowed to his wife.

'My wife is delighted with your work, sir. I must confess I was amazed to hear that you were so young. But many people in Ghent speak most highly of your skills. So, is this it?' He pointed at the covered easel.

'It is, sir.' Johann lifted the cover with care and revealed a portrait of immense calm and beauty.

Oh, goodness! What have I done? thought Johann to himself, as he looked at the panel with fresh eyes in the milky haze of the morning light. *I have painted a picture of some other woman! He will demand to know who this one is!*

The spice merchant and his wife stood spellbound in front of the panel. It was only as they were both held there by the painting that Johann was able to study her face for the first time since they had arrived. He looked back at the painting, then at the woman again. No—it was remarkable! The portrait really was a true likeness after all. Her cheeks were afire with life, where before they had been pale and sickly.

The husband praised Johann's

talents at length. He was clearly delighted. They left, promising to send a servant for the painting in three months when it was fully dry. As the woman passed over the threshold onto the busy street, she hung back and let her husband walk in front of her a few paces.

'He does not know yet,' she whispered behind her hand, a large grin across her face, 'but I am pregnant! Your portrait brought me luck, I think. Thank you.'

How strange of her to say such a thing! Johann laughed to himself when they had gone and he was back in the studio at the top of the house. *Surely a painter's hands cannot possess such gifts?*

Johann stared at the drying portrait on its stand for a moment. A smile crossed his lips as he found the tiny image of himself in the mirror in the upper right corner of the panel. Van Melen and his wife hadn't noticed it, or if they had they didn't comment on it.

He laughed, shook his head and left the studio.

MATJE'S PORTRAIT

'The men say they have not seen you for several days, Johann. What is going on?' Hugo asked gently later that afternoon.

'I have been working on this portrait for Van Melen. He was anxious to see it,' Johann explained, standing in front of the panel.

'Hmm. You shouldn't have worried. I sometimes see him and he never once mentioned it to me. Can I take a look?' Johann stood aside, and Hugo bent towards the painting, straining his poor eyes to see the detail. 'The colour is magnificent. You have captured the natural light from the window,' Hugo said. He paused. 'What's this?'

His hand pointed towards the mirror. Johann was certain he would not be able to see Johann's own image in there. It was much too small for him to notice.

'A mirror,' Johann replied. Hugo straightened his back and looked at the empty space on the wall by the window seat.

'Hmm.' He turned to Johann. 'Well, remember to spend time in the workshop. If you are to become a master painter, you must learn to run the place yourself. The Guild may accept you as early as your sixteenth birthday, you know. Many people are following your progress eagerly.'

'How are you, Hugo?' Johann asked, changing the subject. There was a tiny frown of disapproval on Hugo's face that he had never seen before.

'Tired. I will rest today. Go downstairs and see the men. And Johann?' Hugo turned as he was about to leave the studio. 'Spend an hour with Magdalena this evening. She has missed you recently.'

It was true that Johann had been obsessed by the painting of Van Melen's wife. He had been lost in his own thoughts for days and could not even remember the stormy night when he had finished the portrait. He never had time for friends or fun and he missed his family a great deal,

45

especially on the days when he arrived back after a visit home. Still, he was doing what he loved most in the world so who was he to complain?

Johann spent the evening reading to Magdalena and talking to Hugo about the Italian masters and the great city of Florence. He'd heard the stories of Hugo's visit there many times already, but was always keen to listen to them again.

There was a knock at the door.

'Would you like your supper now, madam?' the housekeeper asked standing in the doorway.

'Yes, thank you, Juyt.' The broad-shouldered woman nodded solemnly and disappeared again. 'I wish she would smile sometimes,' Magdalena whispered and winked at Johann.

One of the other servant girls brought their supper a few minutes later.

'Matje, you may go home now,' Magdalena said kindly, as the servant girl placed a tray on the table. 'You have been on your feet all day. Juyt can clear away. Tell her I sent you, she will not scold you.' Matje smiled shyly and caught Johann's eye. He'd noticed her recently, when she came up to the studio with his drinks or food. She was pretty, although the skin of her face was marked badly in places with spots. He'd often seen her sneaking a look at his portraits or sketches when she thought he wasn't watching.

'Thank you, madam,' Matje replied. She gave a short curtsey and left the room.

The next morning, Johann spent a couple of hours in the workshop with the men, directing their work and setting up two new commissions. It would please Hugo to know they were happy, so this time he would let the men prepare the background for the portraits.

Later, up in the studio, Matje knocked and came in with his lunch.

'Sorry, sir. Madam sent me. She said you might want to eat here.' Johann turned and watched her standing in the doorway, her eyes on the ground. She was perhaps the same age as him, maybe even a little older, yet she seemed in awe of him.

'Come in, Matje,' he said and smiled as she lifted her head and caught his eye briefly. He had never called her by her name before. She came over and placed the tray of food on the table near Johann's easel. As she straightened up Johann saw her sneak a glimpse at the canvas.

'So? What do you think, Matje?' he asked, grinning. Her face flushed red and she hung her head again.

'Sorry, sir. I couldn't . . .'

'Don't be silly. Please, I'd like your opinion.' Johann waited until eventually she raised her head and looked at him and then, cautiously, at the portrait. For several seconds she stared and Johann watched her eyes darting all over the painting of an English shipping merchant who lived in Antwerp, taking in all its half-finished details. Finally she glanced back at him.

'I . . . I don't know how to say it, sir.' Her cheeks were flushed with blood, though it was cool in the studio.

'Try. What do you see?'

'A man. A rich man. A very hard mouth. I don't think he would give his money away easily.'

Johann laughed out loud briefly until he saw her eyes dart nervously to the floor. 'No, you're right, Matje,' he said in encouragement. 'He will find fault with the painting when it's finished and demand a lower price. I'm sure of it. You saw that straightaway.'

Matje smiled faintly, more confident now that he had agreed with her. She looked at the painting again for a moment.

'How do you paint light, sir?' she asked, tilting her head to one side. 'I don't understand how you can paint something that you can't touch.'

Johann stood up and took her arm. She flinched a little.

'I must go. Madam will wonder what I'm doing. She'll think I'm shirking my duties.'

Johann withdrew his hand for a moment. He could see Matje was uncomfortable.

'If she scolds you, tell her I made you sweep the floor. Look.' He took

Matje's arm again and this time she let Johann lead her gently to the table. He picked up the apple from the plate she'd left there and held it up in the air in front of her. 'Where is the light, Matje?' She looked at the apple, confused. But he let her study it until finally she pointed to the left side, where the light from the window touched the ruddy skin.

'There?' she asked.

Johann nodded. 'So you can't touch the light but you can see it. And if you can see it you can paint it, if you have the right paints and know how to mix them.'

Matje sighed. 'I could never learn to do that, sir. It must be a gift from God.'

Johann smiled at her and she blushed a little.

'I don't know about that, Matje. It takes a lot of practice and patience. But I think you could learn. If you wanted to,' Johann said kindly as she turned her eyes back to the portrait.

Johann noticed Matje's face suddenly twitch, as though something had snapped her out of her thoughts.

'I must go, sir,' she said and hurried from the studio.

He didn't see Matje for a few days. In the hours he spent alone in the studio, Johann began to realise how lonely he had become. He knew nobody of his own age. He had no friends in Ghent, as he spent all his time painting. Only on Sundays did he leave the house, to visit home or to go to church with Magdalena and Hugo. The next time Matje appeared in the doorway, Johann was surprised how it made his heart race.

'Madam sent me. She said you were busy and would eat here again, sir.'

'Come in, Matje,' Johann said, standing up and stretching. She placed the tray on the table once more. 'Sit with me. I'd like the company.'

Matje's cheeks flushed. 'I cannot, sir. Madam would not like it. I must . . .' She had already turned to leave the studio.

'Wait.' She stopped and turned back, used to obeying commands. 'I want you to stay. I will speak to Magdalena and tell her you are to bring me my food every day from now on and sweep the room. It can be your break!'

Matje could not help grinning. 'Sir! If I am caught . . .'

'You will not be. Magdalena hardly ever comes up here.' He smiled mischievously and she let out a short laugh. 'You are my servant and I wish you to stay for a while and keep me company. It gets very lonely here all on my own.'

Over the next few months Matje came every lunchtime to sit with Johann and they talked for half an hour about painting, about Johann's old life at the inn, about Matje's home and family on the other side of Ghent. Johann began to look forward to her visits and grew restless as the time for them approached. Each day she relaxed a little more in his company and they laughed together, making jokes about the other servants or the men in the workshop.

'Shhh! Madam will hear me and I will lose my place here!' Matje would say, glancing towards the door. But her eyes were sparkling still and Johann

52

knew she was enjoying herself.

Johann taught her how to draw simple objects like an apple or a tankard and gave her paper and charcoal to practise with on her own.

'I don't have much time to myself,' she said, accepting the paper the first time. But when she returned the next day she had drawn a washing bowl from her room at home.

'You have the shape well. And the shadow, too. Good. Did you have a candle when you drew?' he asked, studying her drawing. She nodded when he looked up briefly. 'So, which side was it shining on?' She pointed to the right side of the bowl. Johann showed her on a new page in a sketchbook how to lighten the shading to show the candlelight and she practised it next to this quick drawing as Johann ate his lunch.

'Perhaps I could draw you?' Johann asked one day. He looked at her face, hardly noticing any more the marks on her skin that could not mask her life and beauty when she laughed. Matje blushed deeply as she saw him looking at her.

'Sir!' She looked down quickly.

'Why not, Matje? Why can't I draw you?'

She was smiling as she kept her eyes on the floor. 'I must go. It is late already.'

Johann drew her anyway. Every day, when she left the studio, he spent ten minutes on a sketch from memory. As he began to add the detail and shade her skin one afternoon, his hand briefly hesitated. Why should he add the marks on her face? Hugo had always been clear that a true artist reflects the world in front of him. But when Johann closed his eyes now and imagined Matje's face he no longer saw the marks at all. Would it be so wrong to simply draw the portrait as he saw her now, in his imagination? *Surely not*, he thought.

By the end of that week he had a detailed portrait of Matje. Even in charcoal her eyes sparkled like they did when she came into the studio and saw him turning to greet her. He rolled up the sketch and tied a piece of red ribbon around it.

When Matje untied the ribbon and rolled out the sketch she gasped and Johann could see her hands tremble. But she kept a tight hold of it and he watched her eyes taking in every detail. The sketch was of her head and shoulders, as she looked obliquely away from the artist. The side of her face that was visible was clear and shaded softly and her eyes glimmered from the light that shone towards her.

'My skin . . .' she said, so softly Johann could barely hear her. For several minutes she stared, unable to take her eyes from the sketch as though caught in a spell. 'My skin,' she finally repeated, a little louder this time. Matje looked away from the sketch and when their eyes met Johann felt a spark, a kind of flame, running through him. 'Why did you mend my skin?'

At first Johann could not tell if she was pleased or angered or embarrassed by the sketch.

Johann was confused. 'I draw what I see,' he said, cautiously.

Matje smiled sadly and looked away

55

from him.

'Do you like it?' Johann asked, gently. She was studying the sketch again.

She nodded and when she looked at him there were tears in her eyes.

'It's beautiful. Nobody has ever given me anything so . . .' But she could not finish. As she rolled up the sketch and hid it in her apron pocket, Johann saw tears streaming down her cheeks and she ran from the studio before he could speak.

The next day Matje did not come. Johann wandered downstairs and entered the kitchen. Juyt was stirring a pot on the open fire.

'Juyt, where is Matje with my lunch?' he asked, casually. 'I cannot work without food.'

Juyt looked up and stopped stirring the pot. The look on her face made Johann realise something was wrong.

'She has given her notice, Johann,' a voice said behind him. Johann span round to see Magdalena behind him in the hallway. 'Last night she told me she was leaving. Her father came early this morning for her money.'

Magdalena took Johann to her sitting room, ordering Juyt to bring him his lunch.

'Sit down, Johann. Is there something wrong? You looked shocked when I told you about Matje. Has something happened?' she asked. Johann wondered if she knew about the sketch, about their friendship. Maybe she knew everything and had sent Matje away. But Magdalena smiled at him kindly.

'I . . . I'm just a little surprised. I thought she was happy here.'

Magdalena patted his arm softly as they sat together on a bench. 'I think she was. But something has upset her. Perhaps we will never know what it was.'

Juyt brought his lunch but Johann wasn't hungry any more. As he picked at the bread and cheese, he wondered why his drawing had driven Matje away.

That night, Johann lay sleepless in bed. Try as he might, he could not understand what had made her leave so suddenly and couldn't help feeling bitterly rejected. She was the only friend he'd made since moving to Ghent and now she was gone, without a word. In the darkness of the room he saw images of Matje's face in tears and a fierce mood descended on him. In the blackest, emptiest hour of the night, when the rest of the world was silent and asleep and all he could hear was the distant rushing of the bitter wind across the fields, Johann rose and stood in the middle of the room in his nightshirt, shivering with cold.

He screwed his eyes tight shut and tried to block out Matje's features. He wanted to erase her like a faulty mark on the parchment so his pain would disappear, but it was no good. He could not bring himself to hate her. He knew that somehow his sketch had touched her soul. But in the same moment it had blown her away like a petal in the wind.

Somewhere, in another part of the city, Matje slept. Johann wondered what she had done with his sketch. Maybe she'd torn it up and thrown it in the river. But then slowly he remembered how she'd called it beautiful and his mood lightened for a moment. Perhaps she had hidden it somewhere safe so that she might remember him when she saw it.

Johann opened his eyes and peered through the window into the darkness. As young as he was, he already knew that he could paint anything with life and colour. One day, his paintings might hang in rich men's houses and guildhalls all over Flanders. Yet it seemed to Johann now that the world was not such an exciting place for a painter—even one as gifted as he. Here, in the deadness of the night, he felt little excitement about his future.

His gift was also his curse, Johann thought. What use was a talent such as his, if it turned people away from him? His one friend in the world had left and now he was alone again, in a city that did not feel like home. For the first time since arriving in Ghent, he began to wish that Hugo had never found the inn on that cold winter's night, starting him out on the path to this loneliness.

THE EMPEROR'S PORTRAIT

In May, a letter arrived bearing the seal of the Emperor. It invited Hugo back to court to paint a new portrait. Hugo consulted with Magdalena.

'Well, maybe one last trip, eh? We could all travel to Brussels; you, me and Johann. It would broaden his education to see the Emperor's collection of paintings. And he could do with some cheering up. He seems to be in such a dark mood these days. What do you say?'

Magdalena was silent for a while. It was not that she objected to travelling. Many years ago she had left everything behind and taken her own children to Brussels for almost a decade, and this was to be a matter of months only. No, it was not the travelling that concerned her.

'Hugo? Please don't be cross, but I must ask you this. Do you still have the powers to paint a royal portrait? You know, your eyes cannot see what they did twenty years ago.'

Hugo gazed out of the window. Magdalena always spoke plainly but truthfully. What he was looking at now was not clear and when he glanced back to where his wife was sitting opposite him on the window seat, even her well-known features were a blur. Only *she* could have asked him such a question. He could never be cross with her. After all, she was only expressing his own concerns aloud. But still, he refused to give up hope.

'I can still paint. As long as I can see the panel, I can paint.'

Magdalena watched his face, as though she was looking for something in his eyes. After a second or two she seemed to find what she was searching for. She touched his arm and smiled.

'Very well. Send word of your acceptance today and I will start the preparations. There is much to be done.'

The smile had already fallen from her face by the time she reached the door.

Hugo's pride gave birth to the last

painting of his career. As he watched Johann help pack his materials into a large oak chest, he secretly resolved that this would be the last portrait he would ever paint. That burning desire to pick up a paintbrush each morning had faded. Now, when he watched Johann working feverishly for hours on end it reminded him of his own youth, but also of how he no longer had the same spirit or energy. Still, one last trip to court, what could be better? There he would complete Johann's education and then bring him back to Ghent, ready to start his very own career as a portrait artist.

The trip was to last three months. The journey to Brussels would take two days and Magdalena was thankful that the trees were already in bud. By the time they returned to Ghent it would nearly be the end of summer. The news had brightened Johann's mood a little. He had said goodbye to his family at the inn, promising to return with tales of court life, hopeful that the visit would provide him with some excitement. His mother had sobbed with pride as she watched him ride away down the road.

When they arrived at the palace they were shown to their living quarters, a series of rooms, one of which had been set up as an artist's studio. Johann still could not believe that here he was, an innkeeper's son, staying in the palace of an emperor. The colours and smells, the giant tapestries on the panelled walls, the long galleries where ladies in fine dresses walked arm in arm, the bustling guards in the courtyard below his window; it felt as though he was watching the visions of a storyteller. He lay down on his bed in the room next to Hugo and Magdalena's and smiled to himself.

Suddenly, there was a knock on the door. When he opened it a boy of his own age stood there, splendid in a red uniform with large brass buttons.

'His Highness, the Emperor, welcomes you to court and asks if you would join him in the garden at four o'clock.'

Johann nodded. 'Thank you.'

The boy bowed solemnly and left.

Johann heard him knock on Hugo's door and deliver the same message. So, he was to meet the Emperor on his very first day at court! Just imagine the tales he would be able to tell on Sundays through the winter months, when his father's customers gathered round the fire to listen to stories of the court of the Emperor. And, what was more, Hugo had promised him that he could help when the Emperor came to sit for his portrait!

'Now remember, Johann. Do not talk to him unless he addresses you. It is a good opportunity for you to observe. Look at the way he holds his head, the dignity in his forehead. Notice his eyes; what have I always told you about the eyes?' It was something he had asked almost every day when Johann first arrived in Ghent.

Johann smiled. 'The eyes are the key to knowing a person's soul.'

Hugo laughed loudly and slapped Johann's back. 'Good boy! Now come. Let us go and meet the Emperor.'

So Hugo led his wife by the hand down the broad, winding staircase, with

64

Johann following behind in his best suit that had been made under Magdalena's supervision especially for this occasion. A servant waited for them at the foot of the stairs and bowed.

'This way, sir. The Emperor is walking in the garden.' He showed them outside. Johann had never seen such a tidy, ordered garden. At the inn, their garden was used for growing vegetables and herbs, and to pen the chickens and pigs in. But here, in this garden, were blocks of neatly trimmed bushes placed around a fountain at the heart of a circular lawn. The sun beat down on their backs as they wandered around, making them hot and adding to Johann's nervousness. Magdalena bent to show Hugo some purple flowers in a bed by the lawn.

'Well, well. If it isn't my old court painter!'

Johann spun round to see a smiling, middle-aged man wearing a green brocade doublet and felt hat. Hugo bowed low and Magdalena curtsied.

'Your Highness. It is my great pleasure to see you after such a long time.' Hugo rose and the man approached and took his hand.

'Hugo! It is good to see you! It has been a while. Tell me, where is your wife?' Magdalena smiled shyly at the Emperor. 'No! Surely not! It cannot be! Your wife would be much older than this!' Magdalena's face was ready to break with the force of her smile.

Hugo laughed gently. 'It *is* my beautiful Magdalena.'

The Emperor took her hand and kissed it softly.

Magdalena blushed. 'Your Highness.'

Johann, standing at the side unnoticed, waited patiently. Finally, the Emperor's gaze fell on him. Johann's body became locked with nerves, as he looked at the most powerful man in Europe. But the Emperor's eyes smiled kindly. Johann thought he saw a good soul shining from the man's eyes. Relaxing a little, he bowed slowly.

'Your Highness, this is my apprentice, Johann. He is already a fine painter. I fear one day soon he will be the finest, and I shall have to give

66

up.' Hugo gave Johann a fatherly smile.

'Well, well! High praise indeed, Johann! Hugo is one of the world's best, you know.' The Emperor patted Johann's back gently.

'Your Highness, I would be happy to be blessed with even half of Hugo's talent,' Johann stuttered nervously.

Hugo and the Emperor exchanged a smile. 'Ah, and modest too, eh, Hugo? Well, that's no bad thing, I expect.'

At that moment a young boy came charging round the corner and almost collided with Johann. He was dressed in a brown doublet and red cap and was perhaps a year or two younger than Johann.

'Philip! This is Hugo. You were only a small boy the last time he was here. His paintings of your mother and I hang in the great hall.'

The boy looked at Hugo without expression, then back at the Emperor.

'I'm bored, Father.' He turned to Johann and looked him up and down. 'Who's this?' he snapped.

'This is Johann. He is Hugo's apprentice,' the Emperor said. 'Why don't you show . . . ?'

'Huh!' the boy said, and raced off up the garden and through a door.

The Emperor looked a little embarrassed. 'My son, Prince Philip,' he explained.

Philip's eyes are as cold as a frost on the studio window, Johann thought to himself.

They walked on through the garden and Magdalena hung back with Johann. Johann heard the Emperor begin to talk about painting.

'Every day I look at the portraits in the great hall, which you painted many years ago when I was still a young man, and I knew only *you* could do me justice. Mind you, I have rather more creases and wrinkles now.'

'Sir, I will do my best and hope that it pleases you. When shall we begin?' Hugo asked.

'Tomorrow morning, eh? Nothing to wait for.'

Back in the palace, Hugo, Magdalena and Johann climbed the staircase, talking excitedly about the meeting in the garden.

'So, Johann. Do you think I can capture his spirit in paint?' the old man asked.

'I'm sure you can,' Johann replied.

Early the next morning the Emperor arrived at the studio. The previous evening Johann had helped Hugo set up a large panel. Now he was busy preparing red ochre for the first line drawings, and mixing some of the base colours that Hugo had asked for. The Emperor was dressed in a long, fur-trimmed red cloak and a gold chain set with sapphires around his neck. He sat bareheaded in a chair by the window which looked down onto the courtyard. Outside Johann could hear the shouts of servants rushing backwards and forwards. Hugo took some time to settle on the composition but finally it was decided. It was to be a three-quarter-length portrait. The Emperor looked away from the artist, his eyes slightly upward and his hands resting in his lap.

'Now, your Highness, I will make some sketches that I can use for the rest of the week as I set up the portrait.

And then I will need you to sit again, perhaps early next week?'

'As you wish, Hugo.' The Emperor glanced at Johann, who had begun to make some quick sketches, as he often did for Hugo's other subjects. 'And Johann? What will he do?'

Hugo looked up. 'Oh, forgive me, Your Highness. My apprentice is used to making sketches of my subjects. It is part of his education. If you would rather he . . .'

'No, no.' The Emperor winked at Johann. 'Let him draw.'

For the next few days Hugo was busy adding the first layers of paint as a background. Once Johann had mixed the paint for the day he was free to explore the palace on his own, or take walks with Magdalena around Brussels. He had never seen such riches and clothes and thought how the city danced with colour compared to the duller tones of Ghent. The large market was even busier than Ghent's, rich with the smell of fresh bread and fish and full of the shouted invitations of the traders. The town hall towered above them, decorated with hundreds of tiny statues. It reminded Johann of the intricate lace that Magdalena had bought to take home to Ghent. Johann made sure he stayed close to Magdalena and the servant who had been sent to guide them. The servant showed them stalls selling English wool, French wine and German beer. As they passed each one, Johann listened intently to the traders who often spoke in languages he didn't understand. Magdalena also found Johann a beautiful leather-bound sketchbook. He'd never owned anything so precious before.

'Thank you, Magdalena!' he exclaimed and kissed her flushed cheek. As soon as they arrived back at the palace, Johann wrote his name in it carefully and stared at the first blank page, itching to make the first sketch there but not wanting to spoil its perfection.

One morning, Johann was alone in the studio when the door was flung open, crashing into the wall behind it. Prince Philip stood in the doorway, legs apart and hands on hips.

'Huh! You!' he scowled when he saw Johann in the corner, mixing vermilion pigment with oil. 'What are you doing?' He strode over and stuck his finger in the newly made paint.

Johann trembled. The boy was younger than him, but he was a prince! He must be careful how he spoke. 'Your Highness, I am mixing paint for your father's portrait.'

'Huh!' The prince studied his finger, which was now bright red. 'It's messy. Wipe my finger,' he ordered.

Johann looked around on the table. There was an old cloth splashed with paint. It would have to do.

'No, not that old rag!' the prince barked angrily as Johann reached to pick it up. 'Give me your sleeve!'

Johann hesitated. Then, slowly, he lifted his arm towards the prince who wiped his finger along the sleeve of Johann's jacket, leaving a long, red smear. Without another word he turned and ran out of the room.

Johann felt humiliated. All his life he had helped his parents at the inn or assisted Hugo in the workshop and the studio. He had never thought himself important, but during his time in Ghent he had gradually learned to value himself and his talents. Never had anybody treated him with such disdain, not even the men in the studio when he had first arrived in Ghent. He didn't like this boy-prince at all. He was conceited and vain. But Johann knew that he must lock such thoughts away.

Each evening Hugo would take Johann to the studio to discuss the portrait, and by the end of the first month the main composition and background were done. But Hugo seemed more and more distracted.

'Are you all right, Hugo?' Johann asked one evening. 'You seem a little worried.'

Hugo rubbed his eyes and sighed, his brow wrinkled with concern. 'Johann. I will tell you a secret. I decided when I came here that this would be my last ever portrait. One final attempt at greatness, before I die.' He stood, wandered over to the window and looked out at the night sky. There were still thin radiant strips of orange on the horizon beyond the palace walls. 'But I am afraid, Johann. I am afraid of failing. My eyes are almost useless, and I think I may have taken on a portrait that I cannot complete to anyone's satisfaction. And it is the Emperor himself. I must have been mad.'

Hugo sat down on the window seat and held his head in his hands. Johann did not know what to say so he simply sat down next to his master. After a minute or two, Hugo looked up and saw Johann there. He smiled and touched his apprentice's shoulder gently.

'Sir, you are already a great painter. You have nothing to prove. The portrait already breathes like the Emperor,' Johann said, trying to soothe Hugo's mood.

'You are a good boy, Johann. You should not worry about the silly moods of an old man. One day soon you will have all of Europe knocking on your door for a portrait. Come. It's getting late. Time for a game with Magdalena before bed.'

But as Johann and Magdalena played, Hugo sat alone in a corner of the room without a candle, his eyes closed. The two players said nothing, but both knew things were not as they should be.

As the successive layers of paint dried, the portrait did not improve. True, it looked like the Emperor, but that was never a problem for Hugo. The Emperor had not been well for the last few weeks, complaining of pains in his hands and feet and aches in his stomach. Perhaps the painting reflected his ill health?

Johann, holding a candle close to the canvas, studied the portrait when Hugo was out with Magdalena one evening at a banquet to which the young apprentice was not invited. The Emperor was coming tomorrow for another sitting and he was sure to ask to see the portrait soon. The skin tones were dull, and the eyes . . . the eyes gave him a look of sadness, rather than his normal, kindly expression.

Standing in the flickering candle-light, Johann let his mind drift so that soon he was only semi-conscious of the face in front of him. The colours floated and shifted, merging together one moment and separating the next. Johann didn't know how long he had been standing there when, suddenly, he rocked back on his heels from the force of a feeling that sprang from deep in his stomach. There, in his mind's eye, Johann could see the very heart of the Emperor's character. He had glimpsed it that first day in the garden when the Emperor smiled and spoke to him, but now he saw it clearly in front of him. And he knew now exactly what needed to be done. His hands trembling, Johann picked up one of the brushes that he was supposed to be cleaning, and began to paint.

The next morning, Hugo put his face so close to the canvas that he could not see the whole portrait at once, but he sensed that something was different. He stood and peered for a long time, grunting and sighing, as Johann cleaned and mixed in the far corner of the room, not daring to look up.

'Johann. Come here,' he said, finally.

'Tell me, what have you done?'

So he knows, the old fox, Johann thought as he approached his master. *Even his poor eyes can see the new brush marks, light as I tried to make them.*

Johann swallowed hard. 'Sir, I'm sorry. I have done a terrible thing. I . . .'

Hugo held his hand up to signal that Johann should stop talking. He laughed, softly at first and soon with heaving shoulders. Johann stood there, confused.

'No, no, no!' Hugo said, when he had recovered a little, wiping a tear from his eye. 'I mean, how did you do it? It's incredible! Tell me how it was done, for I am no longer your teacher but your pupil. I don't know why I didn't think of it before. My final painting should be a collaboration, with the apprentice who is soon to become a master portrait painter!'

Johann was speechless. Only lying in bed that night listening to the excited whining of the palace dogs as they were fed in the courtyard, did he fully understand what Hugo was suggesting.

He was going to help complete the Emperor's portrait!

The Emperor seemed in much better spirits the next morning and laughed and joked with Hugo.

'I slept well last night, and I have woken without pain for the first time in many days,' he said as he came into the studio. Hugo showed the Emperor the portrait and he seemed delighted. Johann could not hear what they said from his corner of the studio, but at one point the Emperor looked over to the table where Johann was mixing lapis pigment with linseed oil. When the sitting was over he asked Hugo what the Emperor had said.

'He was very pleased. He thought it captured his character very well. And I told him, Johann. I told him that you were assisting me.'

Johann grinned. 'What did he say?'

'Oh, he was very happy. He agreed it would be an excellent opportunity to complete your education.'

The last layers of oil paint were being applied. Hugo stood back and watched Johann at work, smiling.

Indeed, here was a true artist and he was happy to have helped him into the world of painting.

'We must mix more vermilion for the cloak this evening, so it may dry a little overnight. What do you think, Johann?'

Johann stood up and stretched. It had been a long afternoon and his eyes were tired. The hot sun outside had seeped through the windows, unnoticed. The courtyards were quiet, the palace dogs sleeping under the shade of the high walls.

'I think it is nearly done.'

Hugo nodded, peering at the painting. 'You have captured his soul, Johann. I could not see it, but you have found it. It may stand you well for the future, eh?' Hugo grinned and slapped Johann's back. 'Now, I will go and see Magdalena, if you will clean the brushes?'

I will clean the brushes, Johann thought to himself after Hugo had closed the door. Hugo had been so good to him that he would willingly clean up for his master. *But one day*

79

soon I will be my own master and then somebody else can clean them.

The painting was carefully removed, three days later, to the great hall where the Emperor was expected to arrive at nine o'clock. Hugo helped Johann arrange a purple cloth to hide it from onlookers. Magdalena, in her new embroidered dress and lace cap, sat at the side and watched as the courtiers began to arrive in a flurry of excited chatter. Johann's heart started to beat rapidly, and he felt hot in his best suit of clothes.

At nine o'clock there was much shouting outside in the corridor before a sudden wave of silence flooded the hall. The doors opened and the Emperor was announced. As he entered, the room bowed as one whilst he sat on the throne and signalled for the doors to be closed. Prince Philip sat next to his father, staring coolly at Johann, who tried not to catch his eye. Then, when the room was quiet, Hugo stepped forward and cleared his throat.

'Your Highness, the portrait is complete. It has been a challenge to capture Your Highness's nobility, but I pray that it is done to your satisfaction.'

The Emperor smiled modestly and waved a hand in the air. 'Well, let us see, shall we?'

'Before I reveal the portrait I must point out that my apprentice, Johann, has helped me to paint it. He is a very talented artist as I'm sure you will see shortly.'

Johann lifted his head and saw the prince staring again. He stepped forward, next to Hugo, and they lifted the cloth from the portrait. Immediately there was an intake of breath from everyone. A long silence followed, as the audience took in every detail of the portrait; the lines of the robes, the tone of his skin, the calmness of the composition. People started to nod eagerly and whisper to each other as the Emperor stood and bent close to inspect the painting. He lifted a finger towards it.

'Please, Your Highness. It will need another six weeks to be fully dry,' Hugo said delicately, not wishing to offend him. The Emperor straightened and stood for a few seconds, his head cocked slightly to one side. Then, slowly at first, he began to clap, louder and louder, faster and faster with each beat. Soon the courtiers caught on and joined in, and before long the room was rattling with applause. Hugo smiled modestly.

'It is truly magnificent, Hugo,' the Emperor said, when the applause had died away. 'And Johann, too!' he added, suddenly remembering and spinning round to smile at him.

'Huh! He just mixes the paint!' The prince had stepped forward, brushing Johann aside, and was looking at the painting carefully. Then he turned to Johann. 'Do you really expect us to believe that you painted this?' he said, and laughed. Taking his lead, one or two of the audience joined in. Johann burned red with embarrassment and looked at Hugo, who could only stand and stare at his feet. Johann knew neither of them could argue with a prince.

Behind Johann, a hand appeared softly on his shoulder, and Magdalena's familiar voice whispered in his ear.

'Don't worry. Your day will not be far away. One day people will know your worth.'

THE PRINCE'S PORTRAIT

They returned to Ghent the next day. On the journey home Johann had been quiet and thoughtful.

'He is tired, poor boy. He needs some rest before you put him back to work,' whispered Magdalena to Hugo, as the coach rattled along the road.

But Johann wasn't tired. As he watched the fields pass by the carriage window he couldn't stop thinking about the prince and how cruel he had been. There was an image of him in Johann's mind of which, try as he might, he could not get rid. And as the rain began to fall on the muddy roads to Ghent, the image was joined in his head by a strange feeling, a feeling Johann had never before experienced. He began to imagine a portrait of the prince in pain, and couldn't resist a small smile.

'What are you smiling at?' Magdalena asked, stroking his dark hair across his forehead as the carriage made its way between the tall houses of Ghent. Johann shook his head, suddenly snapping himself out of his daydream.

'Oh, nothing, Magdalena. I was just remembering something a boy at the palace said to me,' he replied.

Six weeks later, Johann and Hugo returned to Brussels without Magdalena to apply the final layers of glaze to the portrait. Back in the palace studio, there was plenty of time for Johann to use the new sketchbook that Magdalena had found in the market on their first visit. He completed several studies of the hands and faces of servants, who were all delighted to see such a likeness of themselves on the paper. But time and again, especially in the evenings as he stared at the fire, the image of the prince's face came into his mind and would not move. Johann had not seen the prince during this visit, but he began to sketch his face from memory. He tried various angles, but all of them gave a similar result—a conceited face, full of self-regard.

One day, Johann entered the studio to find the Emperor himself sitting alone in a chair at the window, observing the courtyard life below.

'Johann!' he said, seeing Johann hesitate by the door. 'Come in, come in.' Johann stepped forward and bowed to him. 'Come. Have a seat and talk with me,' the Emperor continued, smiling. Johann sat in the chair opposite, but could not think what to say to an emperor.

'We were all very impressed with the painting. Are you pleased with it?' the Emperor asked.

'Yes, sir. Very pleased. Hugo is an incredible artist, sir,' said Johann.

The Emperor studied Johann's face carefully before replying. 'He is, he is. But so are you, I am told. Much of the portrait's success was down to you, wasn't it? You are a modest boy, but you must be aware of your own talent by now?'

Johann nodded shyly. He certainly was confident in his own ability to paint and draw people, but he had not yet found his confidence in their company, especially when it was the company of a man such as this.

'Yes, sir. But I still have much to learn.'

There was a pause as they both watched a cartload of barrels arrive through the courtyard gates below.

'What's this?' the Emperor asked, suddenly picking up Johann's sketchbook, which lay on the small table between the chairs. Johann wanted to snatch it away, but of course he couldn't. The Emperor opened the book and flicked through the first few pages. 'Impressive. Very impressive. I wish I could . . .' The Emperor stopped speaking, his face intent on the image before him on the page. Johann knew he had found the sketches of Prince Philip, and his shoulders tensed as he waited for the outburst of anger that would surely come. But the Emperor simply sighed and shook his head sadly, closing the book.

'You know, Johann. You see the real person in your work. That truly is Philip. You have captured his . . . oh, I don't know what to call it. Spirit? Soul? Character? Call it what you will, you can draw it truthfully, Johann. That is a rare gift.'

Johann looked at his feet. He was relieved that the Emperor had not been angered by the sketches, but he was just as uncomfortable with his praise. 'Thank you, Your Highness. You are too kind,' he muttered.

'Well, how about I commission *you*, eh? Paint a small portrait of Philip for me and I will pay you well,' the Emperor said. He smiled and stood to leave. To the Emperor this was a small idea, a sudden whim, a quick decision made in a few seconds. But Johann knew that in those few seconds his life had changed for ever.

When he'd gone, Johann opened the book again and looked at the sketches. Then he suddenly became aware of the thudding of his heart, as he thought about the most important painting of his short life.

Hugo was delighted by the idea and immediately sent a note ordering a small, ready-made panel to be brought from the workshop in Ghent. He decided that he would wait until Johann had finished the underdrawing before returning home.

'I do not want to leave Magdalena too long on her own. She needs company. I will return when you send word to me that the portrait is nearly finished. Will you be all right, living alone here at the palace?' Hugo asked, looking concerned.

Johann had barely had time to think about the idea.

'Of course, Hugo. You go to Magdalena. I'll be fine.'

The day arrived when the portrait was to begin, and the prince arrived an hour late.

'I hope you really can paint. I don't want to look like a fool, you hear? If it's no good, I suppose we can always burn it,' he said, before he'd even sat down.

The sketches were already made and Johann used them to complete the underdrawing on the primed panel. The prince was a poor subject, squirming and sighing bad-temperedly. He hardly spoke to Johann at all and was always eager to get away from the studio.

Strangely, the prince never once showed any interest in seeing the portrait develop. Johann learned to limit the sittings to one short session a week and in between these he worked on the hues and tones of the background.

There was little free time for Johann but one day he took a break and asked if he could be allowed to see the royal collection in the long gallery. The Emperor, and his father before him, had collected many paintings that Hugo had described to Johann. Hugo had been too hard at work during their last visit to show him.

'Make sure you see them before you leave this time,' Hugo had said, as he left for Ghent.

A sombre man opened the room for him and waited in the doorway. There, in the silence of the panelled gallery, Johann stood amongst some of the finest works of art he had yet seen. Some of the artists he had heard Hugo talk about; Jan Gossaert, Vermeyen, Hans Memling. Others he had never heard of before.

After an hour, the man at the door began to rattle his keys impatiently.

'What about this one?' Johann asked, pointing to a painting with hinged wings that were closed. The man raised his eyebrows and sighed, but took a key and opened the wings.

The painting was about three feet high, a full-length portrait of a man and his wife in a bedroom, with a small dog at their feet. The people seemed so life-like. The whole scene looked like the real world, with every detail seeming to have some special meaning. There were two pairs of shoes lying discarded on the floor. On the windowsill was an apple. There were prayer beads hanging on the wall next to a mirror. A mirror! Johann looked closer and saw the reflection of the backs of the couple. But there was something else, something only just visible in the light from the window that had been painted into the mirror. It was a person, someone dressed in blue, he thought. There was no signature at the bottom of the painting.

'Who painted this?' he asked the

man, who still rested his hand on one of the wings, waiting to close it again. The man pointed to a space above the mirror, where Johann now noticed an inscription. He smiled to himself as he read it:

Johannes van Eyck Was Here, 1434

Six weeks later Johann's portrait of the prince was almost ready to be glazed, and he sent a letter to Hugo in Ghent who returned to the palace right away.

When Hugo saw the portrait for the first time, he was impressed. 'It is an excellent likeness, Johann. Perhaps the Guild will bend their rules when they see you have painted a royal portrait with such skill. Why should they wait until you are eighteen if you are ready to become a master before then.'

Johann smiled but said nothing. In his heart he knew he was as good as any other artist in Ghent, or in Flanders for that matter. And one day he was determined to paint an altarpiece to rival van Eyck's in St Bavo's church.

There was no rush. His whole life lay in front of him. But there was a small part of Johann, a dark and secret part, that glowed with pride at the idea of becoming the youngest master painter the Guild had ever accepted.

'You have certainly got his character!' They gave each other a knowing glance, then laughed, as they studied the scornful face on the panel.

A few days later, Johann put down his brush at the end of a sitting and stood up.

'Your Highness. The portrait is finished,' he said nervously.

'I'll be the judge of that!' the prince replied, jumping up and coming round to the other side of the easel. There was a long pause while he studied himself on the small panel. Then he looked back at Johann with a sneer. 'I don't like it. It makes me look like a silly boy.'

And he was gone without another word.

Deep inside Johann, an intense anger began to boil no matter how hard he tried to restrain it. He stood at the window and watched the prince march across the courtyard.

'But you *are* a silly boy,' he said, his clenched teeth failing to hold back the words.

The Emperor, however, declared himself very pleased with the finished portrait and Hugo thought it the best Johann had yet done. But in spite of the praise, Johann could not stop thinking about the prince's rudeness. It ate slowly away at his insides like a spreading disease.

Late that night, with the palace hushed in sleep and moonlight seeping through the huge windows at the top of the stairs, Johann rose from his bed, still half-asleep, and took a candle down to the great hall where the portrait had been moved. He pushed gently against the heavy oak door and to his surprise it gave way easily. Inside the room he edged his way to the portrait, which remained uncovered in the centre. Johann stopped in front of it, set the candle on the floor and took a grey folded cloth from his jacket. Slowly, as in a dream, he unwrapped the cloth and set it out in front of the easel. From the cloth he took a paint palette, brushes and a rag and began to paint.

He painted no more than a few brushstrokes here and there, so that the prince's expression was altered only very slightly. Nobody but a master would notice the difference. And behind the prince's shoulder, hanging on the wall, he painted a mirror. What was painted in the mirror? The back of the prince's head, to be sure, but also there, like a ghost in the background, was the reflection of the artist himself, a paintbrush in his hand, so faint that it could hardly be seen.

The next morning a sudden commotion woke Johann from a deep sleep. It was still very early, but outside his door he could hear servants running up and down the long corridor, shouting to each other. From somewhere in the palace there came terrifying roars of pain, which had soon woken everybody.

'The prince is very ill! He has the most horrible stomach cramps! Fetch the doctor!'

The court doctor was woken and came running, bleary-eyed and still in his nightshirt, to the prince's rooms. He stayed all morning, ordering servants to prepare this herb or that tincture, feeding the prince medicine from a silver spoon and keeping watch on his pulse and temperature. But late in the afternoon there was still no improvement.

Hugo had gone out to visit the painters' guildhall and meet some old friends. Alone in his room, Johann tried a few sketches from his window but the noise of the prince's pain was too distracting.

At four o'clock, he had listened long enough. Johann took the same piece of grey cloth tied up with string and descended the stairs once more to the great hall. Once inside he opened the cloth, took out a small palette of oils, a brush and an old rag and began once more to alter the portrait.

At six o'clock the doctor left the prince's chamber and announced to the assembled courtiers outside, 'His

Highness is asleep now, and peaceful. I think the worst is over.'

As a sense of calm flowed through the palace, Johann lay on his bed, alone and exhausted. Outside his window, autumn winds chased leaves around the courtyard. In his mind he recalled his daydream about the prince on the journey back to Ghent with Hugo and Magdalena. For a second or two he almost allowed himself to believe that he was in possession of the power to change a subject's life, that he had somehow caused the prince's pain through his painting. Suddenly opening his eyes, he laughed out loud at the ceiling.

Don't be such a fool, Johann thought to himself, shaking his head. He rose quickly and began to busy himself, dressing for dinner with the Emperor.

ANOTHER LETTER

Back in Ghent several months later Hugo took Johann down to the guildhall by the river on a fine spring day. He had never been inside before. As he looked up from outside, shielding his eyes from the sunlight, Johann noticed the same stepped gable ends that had impressed him when he first arrived in Ghent.

Inside, Hugo was shown into a large room and Johann was told to wait in the main hall, in which hung many paintings that caught Johann's attention, including two of Hugo's own compositions. Hugo had already announced in the guildhall that he had painted his last painting, the Emperor's portrait. Now that Johann had finished his apprenticeship and painted a royal portrait of his own, Hugo had spent many hours since their return from Brussels trying to persuade the board of the Guild to make him a master painter.

After half an hour, a stern man came and led Johann into the room. There were about eight men seated around a heavy oak table. Glancing at Hugo, who was sitting at the far end of the table, his apprentice saw an unfamiliar face, set as it was in a deep frown. Johann, painfully aware of the eyes that stared at him, stood at the head of the table as the stern man retook his seat.

'Johann, Hugo has today formally applied to have you admitted to the Guild of St Luke here in Ghent, as a master painter,' said a white-haired man who appeared to be the spokesman for the board. 'We are all aware of your talents. Hugo has provided us with plenty of evidence.' He turned and indicated copies that Johann had made of three of his own portraits that were on a table, leaning against the wall. 'Impressive.' There was a murmur of approval around the table. 'However, there is the small matter of your age. Under normal circumstances a painter must be eighteen before we can admit him to the Guild.'

'Yes, sir,' Johann stuttered, struggling to think of something to say that might impress the men around the table who watched him closely.

'Indeed,' the white-haired man said and lowered his eyes. 'I'm afraid, Johann, that although there is some support for your admission around the table, as a board we do not feel able to alter the rules in your case, remarkable though it is.' He looked again at Johann. 'You are only fourteen, I believe. A master needs not only to be a painter, but to be a *man*.'

Johann nodded. 'Yes, sir.'

Hugo looked up in Johann's direction, although Johann knew his master's failing eyes would not see the disappointment on his face.

'However, we are agreed that a year from today we will review the case again. And Hugo will keep us up to date with your progress over the year, I am sure.' The man smiled and looked across the table at Hugo who wouldn't make eye contact. He was clearly brooding about the decision.

'They are stubborn fools!' Hugo declared once they were outside on the steps of the guildhall. 'I know you are ready or I wouldn't have asked!'

'Well, I suppose it's only another year,' Johann said as they began to walk back through the city away from the river.

Hugo had another appointment with one of his patrons so they parted company in the market square. It was not often Johann had the freedom to wander the city on his own so he took the opportunity to snatch an hour to himself. He meandered between the stalls, amongst the jostling crowds of people. He enjoyed the liveliness and colour, the smell of animals, the stalls where silvery fish lay, glassy-eyed, in rows. He watched the faces of the stallholders as they called out to the buyers and listened to snatches of conversations and arguments. On occasions he took out his beloved sketchbook, trying not to attract attention, and made quick outlines of faces. Johann had just finished a sketch of an old woman's toothless smile when he looked up, right into the gaze of somebody he knew. For a second his mind had to adjust from the image on the page to this new face; a beautiful face with clear, pale skin and dark hair dangling out in curls from under a white cap.

'Matje!' he called. 'Is it you?'

Matje blushed. She shifted her basket of shopping up onto her hip and when she looked back at Johann she was smiling.

'Hello, sir. I hope you are well.'

'Very well. It's so good to see you again,' Johann said, smiling back. 'Where have . . . I mean, what have . . .?' He stopped speaking for a second and looked at her. Suddenly, they both laughed and Johann was reminded of how she used to giggle when he teased her about Magdalena finding them talking in the studio. There was a pause where both were thinking of how to say that they had missed each other. But neither of them knew.

'Your skin, it's . . .' Johann began.

Matje blushed and held her free hand up to her smooth cheek. 'Yes, it must be all the fresh air and sunshine, I suppose.'

'You left so quickly, I didn't get chance to say goodbye.'

'I know,' she said, looking down at the floor. 'I'm sorry.' But she didn't say anything more. Johann told her about the people she asked after.

'I must go, sir. My mother will be wondering where I am,' Matje said, shifting the heavy basket again.

'Please, call me Johann. You are not a servant any more.' Matje smiled gently and nodded. 'Perhaps I could help you with your basket? I am not in any hurry,' Johann suggested.

'No, it would not be a good idea. If anybody saw us and my father found out . . . he would be angry.' She would not catch his eye as she spoke. Johann knew she wanted to stay and talk but he also understood that it could not happen.

'Maybe we could go for a walk one Sunday, after church?' he suggested, but he already knew the answer.

Matje sighed and looked away through the crowds. Above the tall

103

houses the sky was an immaculate blue, the colour of the Virgin Mary's robe. Johann could see the sadness in her gaze.

'No, sir. Johann. It cannot be. My parents would not allow it.'

They looked at each other and smiled sadly.

Johann nodded. 'Then I will think of you often. I will remember your laugh and the happy times we sat together.'

'Yes, I will—I do—think of them also. I still have my portrait, Johann. It is well hidden where nobody will find it, under a floorboard in my little room!'

Johann grinned. 'Good. Then I hope it brings you luck and health and happiness, Matje,' he said.

'Goodbye, Johann,' she whispered, and Johann thought he could see a small tear forming in her eye.

'Goodbye, Matje,' he replied. He wanted so badly to take her hand in his but she turned away and was soon lost amongst a thousand other white caps and women with baskets.

Hugo and Magdalena had already

told Johann of their plans to retire to a house in the country, not so far away. Hugo wanted Johann to remain in their town house and take sole charge of the workshop. Hugo's name counted for much in Ghent and beyond, and Johann's own reputation was firmly established now that he had painted a royal portrait. He would continue to paint from the studio and Hugo would use his own influence at the Guild to gain commissions for the young artist. Now that summer had arrived and the cornfields swayed in the warm breezes, Magdalena reluctantly agreed to leave Johann in Ghent and move out to their new home.

'He will be fine, Magdalena. I will come to town every week and keep my eye on the workshop. He is very well known now, and the commissions are still coming in. And when those blockheads at the Guild realise their mistake and accept him as a master . . . Well, he is a rare talent.'

Magdalena looked worried. 'Yes but, Hugo, you know he's still young. I worry about leaving him alone in the evenings. He's only half a man,' she said.

'Well with his gifts, half a man is enough! And it's a pity those fools at the Guild can't see that too,' Hugo laughed. He only seemed to see the artist. Yet when Magdalena looked at Johann, which was all too rare these days, she still saw the boy.

Johann's star continued to rise. Although Hugo still came each Friday to visit his old workshop and spend the day with him, Johann felt confident in his own profession now. He had yet to see another Ghent painter's work without comparing his own work favourably. The three men who remained in the workshop slowly began to accept that Johann would rarely allow them to do anything more than prepare panels and mix the paint. Other men had been let go, as there was not enough work, so they didn't grumble too loudly. For the first time, Johann began to decline commissions that Hugo might have accepted. He stopped painting banners, designing tapestries or decorations for houses. And yet people were still prepared to pay him well for his portraits. A friendly joke—one that had started perhaps with the men in the workshop—had begun to spread around the city that paintings from the old court painter's studio were somehow charmed or brought good fortune.

Johann missed Hugo and Magdalena's company, especially in the evenings when Juyt and the servants had gone home or to bed and the draughty house was still and quiet. When it grew too dark to paint he would sometimes wander down to the kitchen and warm milk on the fire, like Magdalena used to. The leather-bound sketchbook that she'd bought for him in Brussels was almost full now and Johann would sometimes sit there by the candlelight and flick through its pages. There were portraits of the prince, the Emperor and various merchants and burghers of Ghent and Bruges. There was one charcoal sketch of his own mother which he had completed on a visit to the inn a few months before, hoping to find time to paint her portrait and present it as a gift one day soon.

But each time Johann would soon find his way back to the portraits of Matje, drawn from memory in the days after their meeting in the market. Her face looked silently out at him from the page. He willed her mouth to move, to hear her voice again. Sometimes he stared so hard at an image of her in the poor light of the kitchen that he fancied he saw her move; a little twitch of her cheek, as though she were about to smile at him. Since he'd seen Matje again in the market Johann had thought several times about approaching her father to offer her a better position in the house. He had money now—plenty of it—and could pay her well. But he knew it was just a stupid dream to imagine he could buy her company.

If the weather was clear and not too cold, Johann would sometimes open an upstairs window late at night and gaze out on the labyrinth of streets that stretched out across Ghent. Lights from barges on the river reflected in the murky water but the beauty of it brought him little comfort. Johann would rarely stay there for long. Soon, the welcoming lanterns outside the taverns and the laughter that erupted from inside as their doors opened would send Johann quickly back inside to his lonely bedroom.

When the letter came, it was addressed to Johann, not Hugo. He recognised the Imperial seal at once and tore it open impatiently. The letter was a request for Johann to complete a new commission for the Emperor; a large portrait of his son and heir, Prince Philip. This would be Johann's moment, when the painters' guild would *have* to accept him as a master painter.

He showed the letter to Hugo on his regular Friday visit.

'I'm afraid you'll have to read it out to me, Johann,' Hugo said. Johann had watched him make his way up the street from a window at the front of the house. He walked slowly, with a stick to help him, feeling his way forward for obstacles in his path.

When Johann had finished reading the letter, Hugo sat down carefully in the window seat where Johann had painted Van Melen's wife.

'Well, you must accept of course. I will keep my eye on the workshop while you are away. Not that my eyes can see much these days,' he said with a sad smile.

The preparations were made and a reply dispatched at once to Brussels.

At the palace, Johann was greeted with a respect that he wished the guildsmen of Ghent could see. Johann laughed quietly to himself as the servants bowed to him on the corridors and in the gardens, but recalling his treatment by the prince on his last two visits, he was careful to be friendly to everyone.

'I have heard it said that you can change people's luck with your painting. Is it true?' the stable boy asked bravely, not sure whether he should be addressing Johann directly.

Johann handed him a saddlebag and sat on a stool to loosen his riding boots.

'Well, don't believe everything you hear! Art is powerful; it can show great joy or great darkness, and many things between. But I doubt if it really changes anything much, do you?' Johann laughed at the rumour of his special gift reaching so far afield.

The boy shrugged his shoulders. 'I don't know, sir.'

The Emperor stood as Johann was shown into the great hall, where he had painted unnoticed on that moonlit night almost a year ago. The Emperor walked eagerly forward and grabbed Johann's hand.

'Johann. Good to see you again.' He stepped back and looked Johann up and down. 'My, you are fast becoming a young man!'

Johann bowed low and smiled. 'Your Highness.'

The Emperor ushered the courtiers out of the room with a wave of his hand.

'I want you to paint my son again. When you last painted him here you painted him exactly as he was,' the Emperor began.

111

'Thank you, your Highness. Hugo has always taught me to paint what I see.'

The Emperor looked thoughtfully at Johann before speaking again. 'Yes, but you . . .' He hesitated, unsure how to say what was on his mind. 'Philip is a spoilt young man. I blame myself for that. Perhaps I have not been strict enough over the years. But one day he will be Emperor in my place and . . .' The Emperor stopped and Johann sensed he was about to say something difficult. 'I'm not sure . . .' He raised his hand to his cheek secretively, even though there was no other person in the room. 'I'm not sure that he's ready. Please, Johann, do what you can to help me. Paint him as a leader, a statesman. Or at least give him good grace and courtesy. What do you say?'

Johann was stunned for a second. Quickly, he realised what he was being asked to do, what powers the Emperor assumed Johann had to change the future of a portrait's subject. What could he say? It seemed it wasn't just the stable boy who was convinced

112

of Johann's magical gift. It was true that Van Melen's wife had grown into health and happiness as Johann painted her but how could that have been achieved with a paintbrush? The prince's stomach pains? Well, that was just a strange coincidence, surely. Matje's smooth skin *had* gleamed in the sunlight when they met but it was nonsense to think that such powers could exist in an artist's fingers.

Johann could hear Hugo's advice, the very words he had just repeated to the Emperor, ringing in his ears. He could certainly produce the most stunning likenesses of people but at the back of his mind Johann knew he had not always been honest with the subjects of his portraits. Now it seemed people were beginning to seek out Johann's art for altogether different reasons.

Even if such a fantasy did exist Johann had no wish to help the pompous prince. On the journey here Johann had dreamed of painting tiny pockmarks on his skin or a secret boil on his tongue. On the other hand, he liked the Emperor very much and had no desire to offend him. Words spun around Johann's head until he was dizzy with his own thoughts.

'Well, Johann?' The Emperor looked at him and Johann could see he was desperate for an answer.

'Well, I'm not sure what you have heard, Your Highness. My guess is that you have been told a good story.' The Emperor smiled, a little ashamedly, Johann thought. 'But I will promise you this. I will paint you a fine portrait of a noble prince, one who looks exactly like your son. And then we'll see if it does him any good.'

Johann worked hard for almost three months. The prince, now a young man like himself, was as unhelpful as ever, often arriving late to sittings and sometimes even failing to come at all. He spoke dismissively to Johann, and only when he needed to. But the painting went well. In the evenings, Johann was sometimes invited to dine with the Emperor and his family. The Emperor loved to hear about the progress of the portrait and was keen to hear of the latest techniques in the world of the artist. By contrast, Prince Philip took no interest in the painting at all. In fact, he rarely joined them for dinner.

At the end of the stay, the Emperor was thrilled by the new portrait. In it, the prince sat facing the artist, wearing a red doublet and black coat with lynx fur. A gold pendant set with pearls and sapphires hung low from his neck. Once more, a small mirror hung in the background, reflecting a faint image of the painter himself at work.

Johann was paid generously and the painting was unveiled at a court reception in the Great Hall where he had once painted by candlelight. Prince Philip had poured scorn on Johann's abilities previously and the memory was still vivid in Johann's mind. As the prince looked carefully at the portrait, Johann wondered if the Emperor's son would ever become more worthy of responsibility. He had given him a softer, kinder expression in the portrait, but how would that help him in the real world?

'Johann.' The voice belonged to Prince Philip. Johann turned to see the prince smiling, the first time he had ever witnessed happiness on the boy's face. 'I must thank you. It is a marvellous portrait.' The prince shook Johann's hand heartily. Behind the prince's shoulder, Johann caught the Emperor's eye, who smiled and nodded his thanks.

As his horse clipped over the cobbled streets of Brussels towards the countryside, Johann's thoughts drifted to what had happened. He quickly left the houses behind and headed out on the road to Ghent again. In his head, Johann could see a clear image of the altarpiece in St Bavo's church. He remembered the shock at first seeing van Eyck's painting of God the Father in a red robe. It was a vision of Heaven, so different from all the terrible images of Hell that other artists painted.

Did a boy from a Flemish inn really have the power to change the destinies of princes and Emperors? Anybody with such a weapon in his hands could surely change the world and make it in

116

his own image.

But only God can truly hold the power to alter the paths of people's lives, Johann told himself, and spurred on his horse for home.

THE THIEVES

That spring in Ghent, the Guild had reviewed Johann's case but would still not accept him for another year.

'I told them! He has painted a large portrait of Prince Philip, which hangs in the Great Hall in the palace in Brussels, I said! What more proof could they need of your worth? I have never met such a bunch of ignorant fools in my whole life!' Hugo stormed, when he brought the news back to the town house one Friday afternoon. It took a long time to calm Hugo down and later Johann rode out to the country house with him, afraid to let him ride alone in such a foul mood. It was better to worry about Hugo, Johann thought, than to let his own anger take hold of him.

That autumn Johann began to spend some evenings in the taverns of Ghent, seeking out company of his own age, often returning late at night and sleeping through the mornings. If the

Guild would not show him the respect he thought he was owed, Johann did not feel inclined to play the role of a respectable artist.

'Tell us about the Emperor's daughter, Johann. Describe her like a painting. Is she beautiful?' someone might ask.

For a few weeks Johann enjoyed the attention. 'More drinks, landlord!' he would shout, starting off a cheer around the tavern. As soon as it died down he would begin another story for his audience. He began to make many friends with his generosity as he discovered a new world where people surrounded his table, listening to his tales of life at the Emperor's court. But as his money ran out towards the end of each evening he often found himself the last to leave. After the life and warmth of the tavern, walking home alone through the night, Johann would see the dark silhouette of Hugo and Magdalena's house looming before him, reminding him of his utter loneliness.

As the mists swirled and hid

Flanders from Johann's studio window, he grew more and more dissatisfied with his life. It seemed to him that he spent all his energy and time on making other people happy with his portraits. True, he had plenty of money now. He had servants and a good home. He commanded a certain amount of fame in Ghent, even though the Guild was yet to accept him as a master. Yet he still had no real friends of his own age and it often felt like his whole life was consumed by painting. The people in the taverns just wanted the free drinks and soon disappeared when they stopped flowing.

Slowly, Johann began to sink into a gloom that he felt powerless to shake off. Lying in bed in the late mornings, listening to the shouts of the men in the workshop at the back of the house, his mind raced with dark thoughts; images of the Guild board sitting at their table in judgment; of Matje's tearful face, which haunted him still; of his own parents at the inn, waiting for news of their ungrateful son.

It was at this time that Johann first

became aware of a strange feeling that he could not fathom. Often in the evenings, when he was alone in his room, he almost thought he could sense another presence in the house. At first Johann imagined it must be the servants moving around somewhere downstairs but then he would get the feeling of someone actually in the room with him. But of course when he turned round quickly, there was never anybody there.

One night, lying sleepless and facing the wall, Johann felt the same sudden strange presence in the room. It wasn't a human presence, but a strong and formless force that rang through his ears and tensed his whole body. His neck cooled instantly, which made him shiver all over. For what seemed like minutes, he could not move a muscle, as though gripped by some invisible entity. Johann's whole body was locked rigid. He tried to move an arm, a leg, a finger even, but nothing would move. Then, as suddenly as it had begun, the ringing in his ears stopped and he was released. But for the next few hours he lay in the same position, not daring to move, until he fell asleep in the grey light of dawn.

For several weeks, Johann barely painted anything at all. Again, he neglected the men in the workshop.

'He is never here. Some days we have nothing to do, so we go home. We don't mind telling you, sir, in the hope that you can help us,' one of the men said in confidence to Hugo on one of his Friday visits. Hugo looked around the workshop. A few half-finished portraits stood on easels in one corner, but there was no sign of any recent activity. 'Some days he does not even ask for paint. I don't know what he does up there.'

Hugo found Johann upstairs in bed. Juyt said he had been there for several days and had barely touched his food.

'Are you all right, Johann?' Hugo asked.

Johann looked over his covers and smiled weakly. 'No, Hugo. I am a little worn out. I have a fever, that is all.'

'Would you like us to come back and live here with you for a while until you are better?' Hugo suggested.

'No. That's kind of you but it isn't necessary. The fever will pass, and I will begin to paint again soon. Tell the men not to worry.'

But from then on Johann began to avoid Hugo when he visited each Friday, making up appointments in the city to attend, or pretending to be ill again. For weeks he failed to visit Magdalena or his parents even once.

One afternoon in November, Hugo and Magdalena sat in their parlour talking.

'I worry about the boy. He is already well known for the force of his portraits and by the time he is my age he will be twice as rich as I am. But it doesn't seem to be enough for him. He seems distracted by something, although he says he has just been ill.' Hugo looked across at Magdalena who was sewing, her back to the window to make the most of the weak winter sunlight. She had not seen Johann at all through the autumn, and she missed his company dearly. 'I just hope that fame and fortune do not distract him from true art.'

'Perhaps we were wrong to expect so much of him at such a young age. I blame myself, Hugo. I should have been more like a mother to him.' Magdalena didn't stop sewing as she spoke, and although Hugo's eyesight was too poor to notice the tear that fell on her linen cloth, he could sense her sadness.

'You mustn't blame yourself, Magdalena! It was I who brought him to Ghent and made him an artist. And I'm still glad I did. You only have to look at his portraits to know it would have been a greater crime to leave him in that inn.'

'Yes but . . .' his wife began.

'I know. I forget about the child in him sometimes. I can't help it. It is hard to think of him as a boy when you see what he can do with oil paints. He hasn't had chance to be like other boys.' Hugo stood by the window and felt a cool draught brush his cheek.

'Find out what's wrong. Talk to him, Hugo.' Magdalena said softly, her head still bent to her sewing.

But in his heart Hugo already knew that it was unlikely the boy would confide in him. He knew Johann was avoiding him and if he asked to see a new portrait, Johann would always make an excuse or change the subject.

One Friday, Hugo arrived when Johann was out in the city. He was shown up to his old studio where he sat, staring across to where he imagined the waves crashing in from the North Sea, and fondly remembered old times. After an hour Johann had still not returned, so Hugo rose, intending to leave a note and ride home to Magdalena. But his attention was caught by a portrait that stood, almost finished, on an easel in the corner of the room. Despite his poor eyesight, Hugo recognised his old friend Willhelm straight away. Yet there was something not quite right about the painting, something that for several minutes Hugo could not figure out. Then it came to him, like the sudden shock he used to feel staring at himself in the mirror as a boy. There was no kindness in the face, only wealth and pride and importance. And where Willhelm's long, stuck-out ears should have been were a beautifully formed pair.

'Paint what you see, Johann . . .' Hugo sighed to himself. Now he knew for certain what he had only faintly suspected in the months before. Johann had begun to play with truth. And that was what lay at the heart of the rumours surrounding his portraits. Hugo knew it was a dangerous game, for the world was not made in one man's image alone. Even an artist as gifted as Johann could not master the world. To Hugo it was a sin against man and God to even try. But it also seemed to Hugo that there was little he could do to help if the boy wouldn't allow him. Hugo turned his back on the portrait of Willhelm and left the studio in a fearful mood.

One evening, Johann sat in the corner of a tavern, surrounded by a group of young men and women, most of whom he could not name. Among them were two dark and poorly dressed men, one short and one tall, who

126

said little except to whisper to each other occasionally. Johann couldn't help but notice their sunken eyes and imagine what a wonderful subject for a painting they might make, their pale complexions contrasting with the living colour and warmth of the tavern.

Johann was one of the last to leave that evening and began to make his way home through the deserted streets of Ghent. Down alleys and in backyards the wind scattered buckets and whipped piles of rubbish into brief life. As Johann rounded a corner onto the road by the river, he noticed two shadows by the wall of a house. Before he could make out who they were, they raced towards him. Too late, Johann realised he was about to be attacked, turning quickly to run back to the safety of the tavern as one of the men jumped on his back and brought him crashing to the icy cold road, where his head cracked against a cobble.

'Now, court painter. Give us money!' Johann could not see the face of the man who spoke. He sat on Johann's back as his partner rummaged through

Johann's pockets. There were only a few coins left from the evening in the tavern, but they found his key.

'Ho! What's this?' one of the men cried. Johann knew his head was bleeding from striking the cobble. Suddenly his hair was grasped roughly from behind and his head lifted off the muddied road. Even in his pain he noticed the moon behind a cloud, reflected in the murky water of the river.

'Be still, painter. You are going to invite us to your house now.' He heard the other man laugh as a piece of cloth was hooked over his head and tied around the neck so he could hardly breathe. The men hauled him to his feet and dragged him through the streets. Evidently they knew where he lived without asking because he soon heard the key slide into a keyhole and turn easily. Inside they made him climb the stairs to the top of the house, to the studio where several paintings still lay half-finished or abandoned. They thrust him onto a chair and through the cloth he became aware of the light of a candle in the room.

'So, court painter, this is where you work, eh? This is where you exchange your magic for the gold of the burghers and merchants of Flanders.'

'Please, take off the hood. I'll give you what you want, just let me breathe more easily,' Johann gasped.

There was laughter from both men, but no movement.

'What do you think? Should we?' said one.

'No. He's not to see us. Tell me, court painter, why is it that only the wealthy can buy happiness from you? You make people rich, successful, happy even. But you don't give these things away free, do you? What about a poor man like me? How am I to buy happiness?'

So, the joke, the rumour of Johann's power, was believed by stable boys, emperors and thieves alike. Johann remained silent. He did not want to upset them any further.

'Well?' Johann heard one of the men approach him. The man's face was so close to Johann's that he could feel hot and beery breath through the hood.

'I . . . I could draw you,' Johann stuttered nervously. 'I could draw you both. I could draw you with wealth and happiness.'

There was a long silence. 'And then have us before the stadtholder for robbery once you've seen our faces?' one of them sneered. 'We are not stupid, you know.'

Johann was truly frightened now, and could hardly breathe. He had no idea what they wanted. If they only wanted money why didn't they just take it?

Johann heard footsteps and voices muttering behind him but could not hear what they said.

'Untie him,' one of the men said. There was a pause. 'Untie him. He must draw us, and to do that he must see us. There is no choice.'

Johann felt the ties loosened and then the cloth was lifted from his head. He was in the chair where his subjects often sat for their portraits. On the table were three lighted candles, and beyond that table stood a tall man—

one of the poorly dressed men from the inn.

'So, court painter. Where shall we sit?'

Johann twisted his neck to see the owner of the voice who stood slightly to one side and behind him. This man was short with an unshaven chin. Johann remembered how in the tavern the man's face had reminded him of a bulldog. In one hand the man held the cloth and in the other a long, wooden-handled fisherman's knife.

Johann nodded, his hand on his neck where the cloth had been tied so tightly. 'Good evening.'

The short man with the knife nodded back. 'You recognise us, I see. But you will not know us. We are strangers in Flanders. And when we leave with our drawing, you will not speak of us. If you do, it will be the worse for you.'

Johann understood the threat clearly. For the rest of the night, he was forced to sit and sketch the two thieves in charcoal, chalk and red ochre—just as he had imagined hours earlier—as they perched on a bench together, grinning foolishly and drinking the ale that one of them had brought up from the cellar.

Johann spoke to them, encouraging them to relax.

What kind of men are reduced to stealing other people's gifts? he thought as he drew. *Desperate men, I should think.* And Johann began to feel almost sorry for his captors. Their faces were tense and wary, full of lines and scowls. Was it the Flemish wind and rain that had carved and shaped their faces? Or perhaps they had suffered a lifetime of hardship, which was now etched into their features?

Suddenly, Johann had an idea. His hand began to change routes on the parchment as he stroked the thieves' faces into different expressions altogether. It wasn't sadness, or despair, but something close. He drew their hands in prayer, and their eyes seemed to plead for something from the viewer. And at the last moment, Johann added a small mirror on the wall behind them and hid himself in its darkest corner.

As dawn arrived, the drawing was finished. The two thieves stood before it in silence. The knife lay abandoned on the bench. They had forgotten, for the moment, that Johann was their prisoner.

'Look at us!' the short bulldog said. 'I have never seen such . . . It is something . . . beautiful. How can a man draw like this? It is a mystery.'

The taller thief shook his head in wonder. 'And we have tied him up roughly! How could we have treated such a man so badly?' he gasped, turning to his partner.

There was a long silence as they all stared at the drawing, taking in its every detail. Johann supposed that this was the first time in their wretched lives that they had truly studied themselves.

Suddenly, the short man fell to his knees in front of Johann and grasped at the hem of his cloak. 'Forgive us, sir! I beg you, forgive us!' He looked up, and Johann saw his eyes flooded with tears. Soon his partner joined him on the floor.

Johann looked down at their pleading faces, and a feeling of power surged through his body. He held their futures in his hands now.

'Go,' he said, calmly. The two men stared at him, their faces a portrait of confusion.

'What?' the short thief asked.

'Go,' Johann repeated. 'You have not harmed me. Take the drawing and go on your way.'

The two men looked at each other.

'But our punishment? We must be punished!' the taller one cried. Johann thought for a moment. The first light of the morning was seeping through the shutters.

'Your memory of this will punish you enough, I am sure of that,' he said, and smiled thinly. 'Go now, before you are seen. Take the drawing and it will remind you of your crime.'

With tears in their eyes, Johann ushered the two thieves to the studio door at the top of the stairs. The short man carried the drawing under his arm.

'Thank you,' they whispered, as Johann held the studio door open.

Without another word, he watched them descend the steep wooden stairs and felt a cold draught race up the stairwell when the front door opened. Then it closed again and all was quiet.

Johann looked down at the hands that had just saved his own life. It was only then that he realised they were shaking.

THE SELF-PORTRAIT

The life of a popular artist seemed empty and meaningless to Johann. He was no fool. He knew why he was popular in the taverns, and it had brought him trouble but no real friends or contentment. But it was not long before he felt the need to pick up his brushes again. There was some spirit, some demon at work, that drove him back to his paints.

It was now December. Johann sat and stared at a blank panel as he had done so many times before during his apprenticeship in that very studio. He was waiting for something to strike him; an idea, a thought, an image. And when it finally did, it seemed so obvious!

Who have I never painted? Johann thought to himself. *Why, myself of course. Now, there's a subject. Somebody I know so well, somebody who would appreciate a good portrait. Yes, why not? Wouldn't my own portrait decorate a wall just as well as the portraits of guildsmen and merchants?*

Johann brought a mirror which he placed on a smaller easel next to the panel and began to sketch in charcoal. He worked like a man possessed for the next few days, producing sketches and outlines for a panel. The following week he sat late into the night painting with urgency and passion as the portrait started to take shape. Johann felt an enormous thrill at seeing the skills and understanding he had gained in Hugo's studio and workshop come to life on the panel. For the first time it was as though he was unconscious of the mastery of what he did, something that was beyond the reach of others. There were moments now when he was completely lost inside his work, when his hands and eyes seemed to work independently of his thoughts, moments when he didn't even know where he was, what time of day it was or when he had last eaten. There were even times when Johann felt as though he was somewhere else in the studio, watching himself paint.

On Christmas Eve, early in the morning as he began to apply the last layers of paint, Johann suddenly stopped and considered his portrait. The composition was like nothing he had ever attempted before. He had used candlelight to create a warm glow on his face, banked by menacing shadows. He had placed a book and a globe on a table in the foreground, symbols of learning and experience. The background was simply the unknown darkness beyond the candle. What lurked there, the viewer could only imagine. And the face? He glanced in the mirror then back at the portrait on the easel. It was truly him, Johann the innkeeper's son from Flanders, the felt cap drawn down over his dark hair almost masking one eye.

But the more Johann looked at the portrait, the more dissatisfied he became with it. What he saw was simply a boy; a friendless and lonely boy who had not yet been accepted by the Guild. The portrait was so real that it brought tears to his eyes as he stared at it. It was a reflection of his very soul. Was this what art was supposed to do—to reflect the sadness of the world? Surely nobody would be impressed by someone like this.

Johann sat for an hour or more, lost in the dream-like image of his own face. It was an uncomfortable experience. He saw both the familiar friend and the stranger inside himself, almost at the same time. Then Johann began to think back to other paintings, when he had altered something small, and how the lives of his subjects appeared to have changed in some way. But it had been chance, he assumed. Perhaps his portraits were simply so powerful that they helped his subjects see themselves differently. Until now it had all appeared to be a coincidence, a joke, a myth.

With no warning, Johann's heart jolted and his eyes and mind suddenly broke free of the portrait. Why not? Why couldn't an artist possess such powers? Wasn't art a strange kind of magic anyway? He could tease some importance into the portrait, a superior look in his own eyes, maybe even the satisfied smile of someone who suspects he is a genius. The only person he could hurt was himself and he cared little about that. And if it changed nothing, then nobody would even know what he had attempted.

As the afternoon approached, Johann continued to paint until the portrait began to change; a faint smile and a narrowing of the eyes. With confidence pouring through his veins, Johann jumped up and found another mirror which he hung on the wall behind him. He sat and looked into the mirror in front of him. Now, with two mirrors working together, he could see an infinite number of reflections of his face, each one fainter than the one before, stretching back into a tunnel of darkness. He laughed with excitement. It would be a challenge to paint it. Nobody else had ever tried such a trick and Johann knew that if he could pull it off . . . well, there would be no other portrait like this one anywhere in the world. Once the Guild saw this self-portrait they would no longer be able to ignore him. One day, very soon, he would become the most famous artist in Europe.

A few hours later, when the painting was finished, Johann lit some candles and stood back. The beauty of it! Why had he never thought to do this before? He knew that he had achieved something unique, something truly remarkable. He couldn't take his eyes from the receding tunnel of his own face. For a few minutes it felt like the portrait before him really could save him from his depression.

Outside, the sky became grey as icy rain began to fall in the twilight. Johann pulled his cloak tight around his shoulders. Despite his own fire in the studio, he felt a sudden chill and shivered. Johann left the painting on the easel and went to sit closer to the fire, watching the flames send shadows leaping up the walls of the large fireplace. As he watched, he fell into a daydream.

What a state his life had reached. He should be happy, having just finished what was surely the greatest portrait he had yet painted. He would soon travel again, grow wealthy, meet kings, princes and noblemen. He had already dined with an emperor and he was not yet a master painter. All over Ghent, families would be huddled together around tables with their fires roaring and crackling, the smell of meat roasting. But here he was, alone on Christmas Eve without friends or family to cheer him; only his own genius to keep him company. Among the flames he caught sight of Magdalena's face. He imagined her and Hugo, busy preparing for a Christmas feast, and resolved to ride across the fields in the morning to their house in the country. And there in the fire he also saw the warmth of the old inn, his father and mother smiling back at him. Soon, before the New Year arrived, he would ride back to the inn to see his parents again. Then Matje was there too, laughing as she attempted a sketch in the studio . . .

Johann was jolted out of his daydream as the tree branches outside his window scraped like fingernails on the glass. As he stood to clear away his paints and brushes, there was a sharp knock at the door of the studio. He had sent the servants home for Christmas hours ago. Who could be here, in his house, at his door?

Johann felt frozen to the core and for a second or two his body could not, would not, move towards the door. His spine felt as though an icy finger was tracing its curve. Despite the cold, sweat began to form on his brow. A fear that had no reasonable explanation coursed through Johann's body and he felt suddenly weak and sick as his heart raced out of control.

The visitor knocked again, twice this time. Finally, Johann managed to croak out some words.

'Who . . . is it?' he stammered. There was no answer; just an empty silence, broken only by the drumming of rain on the window. Johann forced his legs to move towards the door, but he had barely taken two steps before his eyes noticed the latch of the door rising slowly. He stopped, stranded halfway across the studio.

The door began to open inch by

inch until a dark figure, some human form, was revealed. It stood perfectly still, featureless in the shadows of the corridor outside the studio.

THE VISITOR

'Who . . . are you?' Johann croaked.

For a moment or two the figure remained still. Johann was just about to reach for an iron poker that rested near the grate of the fire, when it spoke.

'Good evening, Johann. I think you have been expecting me.'

Johann was rooted to the floor. He could neither speak nor move, and ice raced up through his veins in search of his throbbing heart. The owner of the voice took a step forward, towards the threshold of the candlelit room.

The terror still trapped Johann, fixing him like a figure in a painting. He could only watch as the candlelight that spluttered in the draught from the corridor slowly revealed the features of the visitor. He was a young man, of Johann's age perhaps, wrapped in a black cloak of fine quality wool and wearing expensive, well-made boots of brown leather. But Johann's eyes did not rest long on the boots or the cloak. He scrambled backwards to a corner of the room, gasping for breath as he took in the full horror of the man's face.

It was his very own!

The man smiled, a sickly grin.

'Surprised?' he asked. His voice was like Johann's, only as smooth as linseed oil. He stepped into the room, unfastening his cloak, which he threw on the back of a chair before sitting down.

Johann trembled, still cowering in the corner of the room.

'You! You! . . . Who are you?' he croaked, finding his voice.

The young man laughed loudly and the noise seemed to echo through the house. Johann watched the man bend over and loosen the laces on his boots carefully before sitting up again and looking directly at Johann.

'You ought to know the answer to that question.' The young man nodded at the portrait.

Johann's throat closed tight and he struggled to breathe properly. The portrait was still there on the easel.

But where his own face had looked out proudly, only minutes ago, there was now only the black silhouette of his head. He forced himself to creep on his hands and knees towards the portrait, his mind refusing to believe what his eyes were showing him. In the background, the mirror images of himself as the artist were still visible. But the look of horror on those faces chilled Johann to his bones. Each face seemed to shrink back from the canvas, retracting deep into the painting as though trying to escape into the darkness behind. When he forced his shaking hand up to touch the panel, the paint was already dry. How was this possible? Johann leaned back and rubbed his eyes.

'Yes. Hard to believe, isn't it? How can you create a figure *so* life-like that it gets up from the panel and enters your room? You truly are a genius, Johann. There is no end to your talent.' The man, the other Johann, laughed again and it echoed off the walls and through Johann's body, making him feel even more sick.

147

I don't know what kind of monster this is, but it must not leave this room, he thought to himself. *I have caused this . . . this devil. I can't let it loose in the world.*

The man seemed disappointed, as though he could read Johann's mind. 'Oh dear. I sense that you are not as pleased to see me as I expected. Perhaps I am not welcome? I understand. It must be strange to see a living image of yourself. But you should remember I didn't ask you to paint me. And I am here now, no matter what you think of me. It cannot be changed. You have scraped yourself off the panel. I am Johann, the *true* Johann.' He leaned back and crossed his legs. Johann noticed the expensive boots again.

It's true. He is here in front of me. I can't change him now, he thought.

The visitor glared at Johann and rose out of the chair quickly. Still crouching by the easel, Johann jumped to his feet.

'Frightened?' the visitor asked with a throaty menace as he walked slowly towards Johann. 'It pains me to say it,

148

but I have no need of you now.' And with that he lunged suddenly towards Johann. But Johann had half been expecting it and managed to scramble away, towards the door. The man came after Johann, knocking the chair to one side with his hand, his eyes fired with hatred. He bawled at Johann in a voice that seemed to rise from deep inside him. 'Do not run from me . . . !'

'Wait!' Johann shouted, hearing the force of his own voice echo through the house. It seemed to take the visitor by surprise too, because he stopped dead in his tracks. Their eyes locked, as though each was trying to find weakness in the other. 'You cannot kill me!'

The visitor smirked, aware of his own power as Johann stooped with his hand on the door, still struggling to breathe.

'What? I can wipe you away in one stroke. You are nothing now.'

'I mean . . . you *must* not kill me,' Johann stammered.

The visitor watched Johann carefully. Johann tensed his fingers around the door handle, ready to flee if the man tried to attack him again.

'Really?' the other Johann said, raising an eyebrow. 'And can I ask why not?'

Johann's mind was racing as he tried to think of an answer. Maybe he should just run, now, as fast as he could and hope that he could make it out into the street before he was caught by this demon disguised as himself. Johann glanced at his own hand gripping the handle. When he looked back at the visitor, the man was shaking his head, mocking Johann.

'Ah, I see you plan to escape. It is pointless. Your life is at an end, and mine is just beginning, yet we are locked together in a strange kind of way.'

'Yes! That's it!' Johann suddenly saw an opportunity. The visitor dropped his sneer for a moment and looked a little puzzled.

'What do you mean?' he snapped.

'We *are* locked together. If you think about it we are the same person split in two, aren't we?' Johann saw the visitor's face darken, but carried on. 'If one dies, we both die.'

'What?!' the man exploded with rage, and moved closer to Johann so they were no more than a foot apart.

Close up, Johann could see every tiny detail of his face, even the soft, downy hair on his cheek caught by the candlelight. He could almost feel the visitor's breath on his own face.

'You can't *know* that!' But Johann could see he was unsure now. He had sown a small seed of doubt in his twin's mind.

His confidence growing by the second, Johann smiled for the first time.

'Well, true. But there's only one way to know for sure. And I wouldn't want to take the risk. Would you?'

Johann waited and watched. The visitor turned away and walked back to the upturned chair and lifted it back onto its legs. There was an eerie silence in the room as the man sat down. Then without warning he flew up out of the chair and kicked it across the room where it smashed against the wall.

It was several minutes before the visitor spoke. All that could be heard was the storm growing wilder outside and the crackle of the fire in the grate.

'Well, if I cannot get rid of you then at least I can take your place. You are just an innkeeper's son, nothing more. We cannot both claim to be this great artist called Johann. You have created your finest portrait, but—what an irony this is—your career is now over. For now, we must say you are my twin, newly returned from travels abroad, until we find a way for you to disappear.'

Still by the door, Johann sensed a rage racing up from deep inside his stomach and dropped his fingers from the door handle.

'What?!' he shouted. '*I* painted *you*! And with one stroke of a paintbrush I can destroy you again!' He felt the cold sweat on his brow begin to drip down his temples.

The man laughed spitefully. 'How? How can you do that?' He pointed at the blank space on the panel. 'You cannot change an image that is no longer there. Besides, I am no longer a picture. I am real now. Even *you* cannot change that. You have too high an opinion of yourself. Are you even sure you can still paint?'

Johann wiped his forehead with a handkerchief and walked to the middle of the room to face his own image, who continued to observe Johann with a mocking smile on his lips.

'So, you think you are the real Johann? If that is true, then who am I?' Johann asked, calmly.

'You are the old Johann. But the world moves on. Nobody needs you now.'

Johann swallowed hard, as his thoughts took shape. 'Have you thought, perhaps, that you are mistaken? I painted *you*, so surely *I* must be the original Johann. *You* are merely an idea in my head.'

The other Johann's smile suddenly crumbled into a twisted look of scorn. 'Not true! Come, touch me if you need to be convinced that I'm flesh and blood.'

Johann's hand began to reach out. *I daren't do it!* he thought to himself. *What further devils will be let loose if I do? No, Johann. Calmly does it . . .*

The visitor laughed coldly as he watched the hand fall back to Johann's side.

'Stalemate, then. So who is the true Johann? Which of us has the soul of an artist?'

Suddenly, Johann's eyes were drawn to the window. It was dark outside. How long this image had been in the room he could not tell. It felt like only a minute or two, yet the night seemed already well set.

'Perhaps you would like some food, or something to drink?' Johann said. He had to get out of the studio to think straight. His twin seemed unsure.

'Hmm. Well, a little something perhaps . . . but do not try to escape!' he threatened. 'If you do, I will find you. Be sure of that.' The visitor's eyes, even in the candlelight, burned with malevolence.

'Fine. I'll be as quick as I can. Wait here.' Johann fetched two chairs from another corner of the room and placed them in the centre.

Down in the kitchen Johann found some bread and cheese, some ale and a game pie that Juyt had left for him. He stood by the kitchen door with the food and a candle on a tray, listening to his heart thump in his chest. In the flickering candlelight, his thoughts raced. He could drop the tray now and free himself of this nightmare. He desperately wanted to run out into the street, screaming at the top of his voice. He wanted to fly across the fields to Hugo and Magdalena, or back to the old inn, to be anywhere but here in a draughty house that he shared with a spectre of himself.

But something made him stay. Johann wasn't sure how long he had been standing there but when he suddenly snapped out of his thoughts, his heart was slowly returning to a steadier beat. There on the table was his leather-bound sketchbook, lying open in the middle with a sketch on each page; one of Hugo's patient face and on the opposite side a half-length portrait of a smiling Magdalena.

Johann knew he must climb the stairs again and face his torment.

At the studio door, Johann paused. Maybe it had just been a feverish dream? Maybe he would walk in now and the room would be empty and the portrait there, unchanged on the easel? Of course! He was just tired, his imagination overworked from painting his portrait so intensely.

But as he pushed the door open cautiously with his boot, he heard the scraping sound of a chair and saw the image of himself rising from the seat. Johann's eyes flicked immediately to the portrait. The face was still blank.

'Ah. Here you are,' the other Johann said. 'I was beginning to wonder if you had disappeared into the night.'

'I'm sorry,' Johann stuttered. 'It . . . it took me a little longer than . . . I'm not used to getting my own food.' He set the tray down on a table. 'Please.' Johann indicated that the other man should help himself to the food and drink.

As his twin picked at the meagre

offerings, Johann slumped down in the other chair, overcome with exhaustion. Outside the branches of the trees were lashing at the window like a caged animal. He closed his eyes for a moment and saw an image of the sketchbook again, lying open on the kitchen table. Instantly an idea formed in Johann's mind.

'There is a man who could tell us apart.'

The visitor spoke with his mouth full of bread. 'Nonsense! I am the real you. I can tell us apart so I don't need . . .' He swallowed hard and paused. 'Who?' he asked, clearly interested.

'Oh just my master, Hugo. Court painter to the Emperor for many years. He is my teacher, my friend. Yours too, if I'm to believe your claim. He would know the true artist. But you wouldn't want to meet him,' Johann teased. He wanted the idea to come from his twin image. This man was too vain to be told what to do.

'Why not?' the visitor asked, leaning forward in his chair.

'Because he would know me from

157

you in the time it takes to open a door.'

The other Johann stood and flicked crumbs from his legs. 'We must decide soon, that much is certain. We cannot live together. We'll destroy each other. You said so yourself.'

Johann nodded but stayed silent, letting his twin talk. He waited as his other self rose, wandered slowly to the window and looked out into the darkness of the night. The rain still splattered the glass. Then he turned, and Johann could see that he was intrigued.

'Fine!' he snapped suddenly. 'I'm sure it will be a useless journey, but if you think this Hugo can solve the argument then let us go to him now and see.' He grasped his cloak, eager to end the dispute.

'What? Now? You have seen the weather tonight. It is not fit for travelling,' said Johann, alarmed.

'It must be now, before dawn breaks,' replied his other self, buttoning the cloak up to his chin.

And Johann, too, knew they must travel the muddy road to Hugo's house

in the country and wake him in the
dead of night.

THE JOURNEY

The streets of Ghent were empty as they slipped quietly out of the front door and onto the cobbles. Only the wind chased and whipped raindrops around the tall, gabled houses.

'This way,' Johann indicated the road. 'Although I expect you already knew that?'

The other Johann sneered at him. 'You expect me to walk?'

'Did you come by horse? Perhaps you left it somewhere close by?' Johann joked. Now he was out of the house he felt a sense of relief relaxing his whole body. The visitor snarled at Johann, his eyes flashing with disdain. 'Anyway,' Johann continued. 'It might help to clear our heads.' He walked on, and a moment or two later heard the footsteps of his malevolent twin behind.

The journey from Ghent through the foul night quickly left Johann wet and cold, with his old boots caked in

160

clinging mud. They walked for an hour in silence, with only the howling wind in their ears. The roads were often flooded and they had to climb into the fields to skirt around the water and mud. Twice they lost a smaller road in the darkness and had to retrace their steps to find it again. Yet the other Johann didn't seem to feel the cold. Where Johann's fingers curled numbly inside the sleeves of his jacket and his whole body shivered against the icy wind, his double appeared not to notice the weather. He only complained about his clothes becoming dirty.

'This is a cunning trick! You are ruining me so this Hugo won't believe I am who I am!' Johann's twin gasped, as he wrenched his expensive boots free of the mud.

That's not my plan, although if you stumbled away into the darkness for ever, I would be relieved, Johann thought to himself as he peered into the night, looking for the road to Hugo's house. What Hugo might actually be able to do to help when they arrived, Johann wasn't really sure. Was this just an

161

image next to him; a reflection or a real man? In the depth of this winter night, Johann no longer knew his own mind. But he had no other choice. He had to trust that Hugo would have an answer.

Sometimes, Johann thought he could see lights out there in the darkness, but then they would disappear again as he blinked to clear the rain from his eyes. The fields seemed full of black ghosts and shadowy demons skulking, waiting for Johann to fall down in the mud. Each outline of a leafless tree appeared to him as a bony, demented hand, waving in the gale. Again, he began to doubt if the other Johann was real. Perhaps he was a vision or nightmare brought on by fever or exhaustion? But when he looked behind him, the visitor was always there, distracted by the state of his clothes and boots.

'My boots!' Johann heard him mutter, as he stopped and leaned against a tree and attempted to clean them with a clump of wet grass.

'We will never get there if you keep stopping!' Johann shouted through the wind, but his twin did not answer, or even look at him. 'Come! I'm half-frozen. We must keep moving.'

Eventually the other Johann caught up.

'Where now, painter? Are we lost?' he sneered. 'Or are you planning another swamp for us to walk through? We've walked so far we must be nearly at the sea.'

'No, we are not lost, but it's difficult to see the way. The road to Hugo's house is nothing more than a track, and in this weather and darkness it's not easy. We should have waited until morning.' Johann battled ahead and heard his companion follow, grumbling under his breath.

By now, Johann was exhausted. The long journey through the wild night had drained him of all energy. On seeing another light in the blackness, Johann lurched towards a gap in the hedge and fell. His head struck something hard and rough and he felt a searing pain.

'Ha! You see?' Lying there with his cheek on the cold mud and his eyes closed, Johann heard his own voice above him, mocking. 'You cannot even

163

walk now! You are finished. Admit it!'

For a moment, Johann lay there, not moving. Something warm trickled down his face. He could just lie there and wait for this nightmare to finish, go to sleep in the mud and the rain and wake up in his own bed. He even felt a little warmer now.

'Johann!' He heard his own voice again, although it seemed a long way off. Johann smiled to himself as he saw a picture in his head of his mother and father at the inn. 'Johann! Come on, man! You cannot leave me out here in the darkness! I don't know my way!' The voice seemed closer now. Johann opened his eyes and with a great effort turned over and began to sit up.

'Come on, let me help you.' Johann looked up to see his twin offering his hand. He looked scared—perhaps he did believe that one Johann could not exist without the other?

'No! Don't touch me.' Johann hauled himself to his feet, though his head throbbed and his legs felt heavy. He felt his head where the rock had split his skin and looked at the blood on his finger. Johann's twin watched in silence.

'Come on.' Johann began to trudge on through the darkness.

Finally, through the driving rain and the manic swaying of a copse of trees, Johann spotted the dark outline of a house. He waved his companion on and as they got nearer, Johann was relieved to see the lifeless, shuttered windows of Hugo and Magdalena's home. There was no sign yet of the light of Christmas morning in the sky to the east, but it could not be long now. Johann was so tired and weak from the walk, he felt as though he might collapse at any moment.

The other Johann stood back and looked at the house. 'Finally! I hope this Hugo has servants to clean my boots and dry my cloak. I can only imagine how terrible I must look.'

But Johann saw how untouched he was by the night's journey. He did not shiver with cold. The rain seemed to run straight off his cloak and his boots, although a little muddy, were not soaked like Johann's.

'We should wait here until sunrise. We cannot wake him at this hour,' whispered Johann, leaning against the wall of the house.

But the other Johann had no such concerns. 'Don't be stupid, painter! You will freeze to death standing out here. It must be now, before daybreak.' He seemed to be in a hurry. He bent down, picked a small stone from the ground and hurled it at an upstairs window. 'Ho! Court painter!'

A moment or two later they heard the window slide up and the shutters open. Hugo's head appeared, squinting against the lashing rain.

'Who's there?' he hissed angrily.

'Johann,' his twin called out imperiously.

Hugo grunted softly, both relieved and confused by the news. 'What is it, Johann? It's not yet dawn, you know!'

Johann signalled the other to be quiet so he could answer his old master. 'I am so sorry to wake you at such an hour, but there is something important I need your help with. It cannot wait.'

166

'Wait there. And be quiet. Magdalena is asleep still.'

A few minutes later they followed Hugo's candle into the parlour at the back of the house. He turned and faced them.

'So, Johann. What is it?' he asked, impatiently.

'It is a long story . . .'

Johann recounted the events of the night so far. Hugo listened, murmuring occasionally and sighing once or twice. Only at the arrival of the twin did a change appear on Hugo's face. It was a look of horror.

'So, where is he now, this other you?' he asked.

At that very moment Johann's heart sank. Hugo could not even see the other man who stood silently in the shadows. In fact, he could no longer see anything at all.

MIRROR IMAGES

There was a long silence as Johann took in the significance of Hugo's blindness. If he could not see, how would he tell them apart?

'You are referring to me, I believe?'

Hugo spun round towards the owner of the voice as he stepped forwards from the darkness.

'What the devil . . . ?! Johann?'

The man laughed. 'We do not know who should answer you, sir. Should it be me? After all, I am the true Johann.' He turned and looked at Johann with derision. 'There. I told you it was a useless journey. Your master cannot see a hand in front of his own face. How could he tell us apart? Come, we shall go and find another way.' His grin twisted his mouth with malice.

Oh no, you don't fool me, Johann thought to himself. *Hugo cannot see, but Magdalena can. She loves me like a son. She will know me.*

'No, Johann!' Hugo replied when

it was suggested he wake Magdalena from her bed. 'Absolutely not! I will not allow her to become involved in this . . . this devilry! And on this most sacred day. No, there is another solution, which I think will make things clearer to us all.'

Hugo hobbled over to a cupboard and opened it, feeling around inside it until he had found what he was looking for.

'What are you doing?' Johann's twin said nervously. 'I warn you! Do not try and trick me!'

Emerging back in to the candlelight Hugo passed an object to Johann. It was a small mirror, with a black pearl frame and handle.

'Here. You first. What do you see?'

Johann almost recoiled with disgust when he looked in the mirror. The extra candles that Hugo lit did not help much and the image was dim. His hair was plastered to his skull by the rain, and his sunken cheeks had no colour. Blood and mud streaked his temples and forehead. It was like staring at a lesser version of himself,

169

a faded painting damaged by sunlight. His features seemed contorted in the flickering, ghostly half-light of the candles. The mouth was twisted down giving him an ugliness he had never seen in his reflection before. And his eyes; dark, cold eyes that betrayed his pride stared back at him from the mirror. Johann was horrified by what he saw, so much so that for a long time he could barely speak. But then, as the first strip of daylight appeared across the fields, Johann began to describe himself.

When he had finished an expectant silence hung in the room. The wind outside had given up its battle with the window panes. Eventually, Hugo stood and spoke. His voice was grave as he took Johann's hands in his.

'I am glad you still have the words of a true portrait painter to describe what you see. If it is *you*, Johann, then all is not lost.'

Johann felt Hugo's hands begin to warm his skin. For a moment he felt as he had once, many years ago, a small boy standing in deep snow outside the inn, protected from the harsh world by his own father's hands.

Hugo released Johann and turned round. 'And now, sir. Your turn.'

The other Johann seemed nervous and unusually quiet. Outside, the day was gaining ground on the stormy night they'd travelled through. He stretched out an unsteady hand to take the mirror from Hugo. He held it before him, and gasped.

'Tell me, what do you see? Is it the same?' Hugo asked.

The other Johann stood and stared at the mirror for, as it seemed to his creator, an age.

What does he see? Johann wondered. He was desperate to creep round behind and look over his shoulder. But Johann looked across at Hugo and saw him waiting patiently and decided to do the same.

Then, suddenly, a tiny shaft of corn-coloured sunlight pierced the window. Johann watched as his creation twisted his head towards it, then drew back his hand and flung the mirror at the fireplace where it smashed into tiny fragments.

'Nothing! I see . . . nothing!' he screamed, and began to inspect his hands with a look of horror on his face. Then, in a blind panic, he ran his fingers over his features, as if trying to reassure himself that he was still there. 'What *am* I, that has no reflection?'

As he spoke the sunlight seemed to darken his tone instead of lightening it. The day crept forward by inches into the room and the outline of Johann's twin began to blur, his features blending together like thinned oil paint until they were only an indistinct shadow like an underpainting. As Hugo stood and waited, a heavy silence carpeted the room. Minutes passed, and nobody spoke. Finally, Hugo reached out a hand to search for Johann, the real Johann, the one who he supposed was still in the room. But he found only air.

'Johann?' he called. There was no answer. Upstairs, he could hear Magdalena stirring in the bedroom. 'Johann!' In desperation to find his apprentice in the room, Hugo began to stagger from wall to wall, stumbling into chairs. 'Johann!' he cried again.

For a second or two, imagined pictures of the last few minutes tumbled inside Hugo's head, as he tripped over something, lost his balance and collapsed in a heap by the door. He heard Magdalena coming down the stairs. Putting out his hand to lift himself up he brushed against something soft and warm. Hugo realised he was touching skin.

'What on earth is all that noise?' Magdalena said as she tried to push the door open, only for it to be blocked by some heavy weight behind.

'It is Johann, Magdalena,' replied Hugo, getting to his feet. 'He has collapsed.'

A NEW YEAR

In the darkness of the early hours of the mornings, with the candle long burned out, Magdalena would fall asleep briefly in the chair by Johann's bed. His cries would jolt her awake from time to time and she would wipe his brow with cool water from a basin. His terrors seemed to be worse when the wind blew strongly from the west, as they often did in the winter, although she sometimes wondered if that was just her imagination. What a powerful thing the imagination was, she thought. Hugo would take over as the first light appeared through the small window, sending her away to her own bed to rest. But she could rarely sleep there for worry. There had been nights when she was sure Johann would slip away into darkness for ever. He opened his eyes occasionally, but never saw her. His skin was white as the snow that had fallen after Christmas. And hot, so very hot that she brought some in from the garden to cool him.

Then, after several days and nights of fever, Johann began to sleep more soundly. One morning, Hugo sat in the chair by the bed, listening to the rhythm of his apprentice's breathing. Magdalena had finally fallen asleep, happy that Johann's fever seemed to have burned itself out. When the rhythm changed, Hugo knew Johann was awake.

'Where is he?' Johann's voice cracked as he spoke.

'He's gone, Johann. You have sent him away.'

There was a long pause before Johann spoke again. 'No. It was not my work. It was you who could see me clearly, Hugo. You sent him away.'

The two men sat until the sun streamed through the window and Magdalena found them there together. They talked of past times and, of course, painting. Johann described the loneliness and despair of the last few months of his life.

'Perhaps it is my fault,' Hugo said, when Johann had finished.

'How can it be?' Johann replied, anxious not to upset the old man any further.

'I took you from your parents when you were still a child. I treated you like an adult when you should have still been playing in the fields.'

Johann shook his head, though he knew Hugo could not see. 'No. You were never anything but good to me, Hugo. You and Magdalena have been like parents, and have given me a life I could only have dreamed about in my little room at Father's inn.' He smiled warmly at Magdalena. 'No, I cannot let you think that. I know now what I must do, how I must paint. Thanks to you, Hugo.'

Hugo smiled and placed his hand on Johann's. 'Good. I'm glad. And in a week or so, when you are strong again, you must ride home and see your parents. It is a new year, after all. And I think before too long you should paint another self-portrait. It will help to rid you of your fears. Only this time . . .' Hugo began.

'I know. Paint what you see, not what

176

you want to see.'

Johann returned to Hugo's house in the spring and stayed for a month, delighting Magdalena who had missed him dearly. In the early mornings and late afternoons, when the light was at its best, Johann painted himself again. Only this time he sat with Hugo, who talked about his memories of his apprentice, how he'd first found that precious little charcoal sketch at his father's inn, about portraits they'd painted, mistakes they'd made. And as they talked, Johann realised he was painting himself as he really was.

When the portrait was finished, they showed Magdalena.

'It is you. It really *is* you, as though you'd walked into the painting,' she sobbed through tears of joy.

She embraced him warmly and kissed his forehead. And when she'd gone, Hugo found Johann's hand and held it firmly.

'We'll take this to the Guild when it is dry. They'll see now that you are ready for greatness,' he said, smiling.

Johann placed his free hand on top

and laughed gently. 'It doesn't matter, Hugo. Not any more. I have a whole lifetime of painting in front of me.'

'But they should see . . .' Hugo began.

'No, Hugo. I know you want what's best for me, but from now on my portraits will speak for themselves. And anyway, it isn't long to wait now.'

Hugo nodded as Johann helped him up and took him by the hand and led him to the open window.

'Can you see the shapes of the clouds, still?' he asked.

'No, Johann. It is many months since light passed into my eyes. But I still see pictures in my head. I can still feel the air on my face and imagine the cornfields swaying. I cannot see you, or your portrait, but I can feel both. And it is a good feeling I have.'

They stood there for a long time in comfortable silence, as the sunlight slowly dripped beyond the horizon like syrup. And each knew that the other was composing a new painting in his head.

EPILOGUE

Did you look in that mirror?

What did you see? All you can say for certain is that the nose there is your nose, the freckles are your freckles. You can't do anything much about them.

Did you look long and deep into your own eyes, though? Did you find that strange face staring back at you? If you did catch a glimpse, be very careful, whatever you do. You don't know what this stranger is like. It may be your face, but is it really you?

Now there's a question . . .